World's Fair Commission, Herbert C. Gregg

Idaho

gem of the mountains

World's Fair Commission, Herbert C. Gregg

Idaho
gem of the mountains

ISBN/EAN: 9783337291266

Printed in Europe, USA, Canada, Australia, Japan

Cover: Foto ©Andreas Hilbeck / pixelio.de

More available books at **www.hansebooks.com**

IDAHO—

Gem of the Mountains

OFFICIAL

BY
HERBERT C. GREGG

SOUVENIR

IDAHO WORLD'S FAIR BUILDING

— PUBLISHED FOR AND BY AUTHORITY OF

IDAHO WORLD'S FAIR COMMISSIONER

PRICE 50 CENTS

ILLUSTRATED UNDER DIRECTION OF
T. McWHORTER

1893
PIONEER PRESS COMPANY
ST. PAUL, MINN.

JAMES M. WELLS.

INTRODUCTION·

THE task of collecting an exhibit in the State of Idaho for the Columbian Exposition has not been an easy or an envious one. Beginning his labors fully a year behind every other state, and handicapped during the first year with the very small and inadequate appropriation of $20,000, the commissioner was obliged from the very outset to make the subject of economy a study rather than to devote his energies to efficiency and rapidity of work; and it was not until an additional appropriation of $30,000 was made, on the first of February, 1893, that the plans laid out by the commissioner for a proper representation of the state could be prosecuted with anything like vigor or certainty. Whatever has been done in the interests of Idaho at the Columbian Exposition has been mainly accomplished since that date. And this appropriation was asked, not as the estimated amount it was believed to be necessary to successfully carry out so vast an undertaking, but it was the very highest sum which it was thought possible to obtain through the legislature. An additional $5,000 asked for would undoubtedly have proved fatal to the measure, and no money at all would have been appropriated. Experience had already taught that the feeble powers of any one man were altogether inadequate to raise any considerable sum for World's Fair purposes by private or voluntary subscriptions, excepting, perhaps, through the liberality of a few individuals. But the task of collecting Idaho's exhibit has been rendered difficult for many reasons other than those given above. In the first place, there was very little material at hand with which to begin. Scarcely a county fair had ever been held in the state, and everything in the form of an exhibit had to be dug from the ground and taken from the stump. It must be borne in mind, in this connection, that there is not in the whole state an organization of any kind for the promotion of such a work; not a stockbreeders', agricultural, horticultural, pomological or other association existing anywhere, and not a scientific man engaged in any of these studies or pursuits. Consequently the commissioner found at his command no collection made and no machinery at his disposal ready to be set in motion, as in other states, for the better and more ready accomplishment of an undertaking far-reaching in its scope and promises, and of vast importance to the state, when viewed in the light of its probable results. In addition to the difficulties above enumerated, the commission has been called upon in the very limited time allowed for the work, to withstand the losses incident to two fires and two bank failures. In the first instance, many of the choicest exhibits from Latah County were destroyed when the town of Kendrick burned. Following this came the burning of a full carload of agricultural exhibits, taxidermy and paintings while in transit, and this, after every expense incident to their collection and shipment had been paid. While the intrinsic value of these exhibits would not count up into the thousands, still the loss to the state, inasmuch as they cannot be replaced, is very great, and can hardly be estimated by monied values. A pavilion for their reception in the Agricultural building had already been erected at great expense. Among other things in the car burned was a large oil painting by Mr. McMeekin of Salmon Falls. This painting was somewhat damaged by fire, but not necessarily destroyed. It had been loaned to the state for exhibition purposes. Other exhibits destroyed were from Latah, Nez Perce, Washington and Ada counties. The next great calamity was the failure of the bank at Wardner, in which the Ladies' Columbian Club of that place was victimized to the amount of $500. This was a great loss to us as well as to the ladies of Wardner, it virtually being so much money taken from the state's limited appropriation. Following close upon the heels of this comes the still greater loss of $1,543.59, through the failure of the Columbian National Bank at Chicago. It was expected, and it is a fact, that exhibitors are filched and bled here with overcharges on every hand. Still, it was not expected, and there seems to have been no way of anticipating or guarding against wholesale robberies of this kind.

When the labor and anxiety incident to the raising of the legislative appropriation is considered, and at the same time taking into account the lack of interest manifested by the people everywhere, the discouragements of the commission have been at times somewhat appalling, and only for the very liberal terms granted by the Union Pacific road, Idaho's exhibit at the World's Fair must have, in some respects, proven a failure. Something like $5,000 of the state's appropriation had been paid to this road for freights on material for the Idaho state building. The long distance from home, and the slow process of drawing warrants on the state treasury, made it impossible for the commissioner to meet his immediate and pressing obligations, after the losses by the bank, and there seemed to be no possibility of tiding over this emergency except through the assistance of the railroads. Accordingly the circumstances were presented to President Clark of the Union Pacific, who, without hesitancy, indorsed a recommendation to Mr. J. A. Munroe, general traffic manager, for a rebate to the Idaho commission of all moneys paid for freights over their road, and the commissioner has already deposited to the credit of the state something over $5,000 on this account. This liberality on the part of the Union Pacific Company, just at this critical juncture, has been of inestimable value to the state. Notwithstanding all the difficulties encountered, the work of Idaho's exhibit has gone steadily on, and to-day its complete and triumphant success is assured. At this writing (June 1st) there are on an average from 5,000 to 10,000 people passing through the Idaho state building every day in the week, viewing with wonder and astonishment its material and construction. While this is going on, fully as many more, with equal amazement and admiration, are viewing our exhibit of fruits at the Horticultural building, which is universally conceded to be one of the very best, if not the finest, exhibit of fruits at the World's Fair. Heretofore but little has been said of our mineral display, for the reason that circumstances have been such as to make it impossible to get the exhibit in place. To-day, however, the curtains are lifted, and over 7,000 specimens of the richest ores of the state, properly classified and displayed in an artistic manner, and surrounded by an elegant pavilion, are being admired, criticised and analyzed by tens of thousands of visitors daily. Further down, and at the southern extremity of the grounds, Idaho is displaying the finest timbers to be seen from any state or country. It is a fact, then, that our little state, heretofore unknown, unhonored and unsung, is being heralded daily in favorable comment by thousands of people, and in every print, throughout the United States and the civilized world.

COLUMBIAN COMMISSIONER FOR IDAHO.

JAMES M. WELLS, Columbian Commissioner for Idaho, was born in Erie County, State of New York, but moved to Michigan with his parents at the early age of two years, where he was raised on a farm and educated in the common schools. Seized with the spirit of adventure he left school and crossed the plains in 1860, remaining at Virginia City, Nevada, something more than a year. On the eleventh day of August, 1861, he sailed for his home in Michigan, where, in December of that year, he enlisted as a private soldier in the Eighth Regiment of Michigan Cavalry. He participated in the celebrated Morgan raid through the states of Kentucky, Indiana and Ohio, being present at the capture of that noted rebel chieftain. He was also with his regiment through the campaigns of East Tennessee, Atlanta and Nashville, and was promoted meantime to the rank of captain. Captain Wells was twice a prisoner of war, and was entertained in three Southern prisons. He was one of the party to pass through the historic tunnel at Libby Prison, Richmond, Va., and was among the 48 prisoners who made good their escape at that time. Returning to his regiment, he was captured near Athens, Ga., in August, 1864, on the celebrated raid led by General Stoneman, for the purpose of releasing the Federal prisoners at Macon and Andersonville. In common with many other officers of this command, Captain Wells was placed under fire of the Federal batteries at Charleston, S. C. From Charleston he was exchanged and mustered out at Pulaski, Tenn., July, 1865. In 1868 he emigrated to Mississippi, receiving an appointment by the general government in the internal revenue service, and subsequently served as a writer on several different daily newspapers. From Mississippi, in 1877, the subject of this sketch moved to Washington, D. C., where he filled important positions in the War Department and United States Treasury under Secretaries McCreary, Sherman and Windom. In 1884, being broken in health from disease contracted while a prisoner of war, he emigrated to Idaho and settled on a ranch, where he still lives.

Mr. Wells was a member of the First Legislature of Idaho, where he served in the State Senate with honor and distinction. He was strongly urged to become a candidate for governor on the Republican ticket at the November election in 1892, but declined the nomination, preferring to carry out the work of representing Idaho at the Columbian Exposition.

HISTORICAL.

THE State of Idaho comprises a part of the vast territory lying west of the Mississippi River acquired by cessions, by treaty, from France in the year 1803, and from Spain in 1819. The superior right of Spain to territory west of the Rocky Mountains, adjacent to the Pacific Coast, appears to have been recognized by the Treaty of Utrecht as early as the year 1713, to which England, France and Spain were signing parties. The right of Spain to the exclusive sovereignty to all the possessions she claimed on the Pacific Coast was guaranteed to her. In 1789 Spain erected fortifications on an island in Friendly Cove in Nootka Sound. By the Treaty of Escurial, signed in 1790, the rights claimed by Spain were undisturbed, and England acquired no sovereign rights on the coast, but obtained for her subjects the same rights to become traders as those of other nations.

Immediately after the cession by France, an expedition was organized, by order of President Jefferson, under the auspices of the United States Government, for the purpose of exploring the unknown regions between the Mississippi River and the Pacific Ocean. The expedition, in charge of Captains Meriwether Lewis and William Clarke, of the United States Army, started in May, 1804, and spent the winter on the Missouri River, in the present State of Montana. On Sept. 11, 1805, the party commenced the passage of the Bitter Root Mountains, and on the twentieth they reached an Indian village of the Nez Perces, about 15 miles from the South Fork of Clearwater River. On Nov. 14, 1805, the expedition, after much suffering for want of food and extreme hardships, arrived at the mouth of the Columbia River. Fortifications were erected on the south side of the river, a few miles from its mouth; the works were finished on the evening of Dec. 31, 1805. Here they remained until March 23, 1806, on which day, after posting a written notice of their overland exploration, the party started on its return trip over the same route it had come, and arrived at St. Louis in September, 1806. The doubtful claim of sovereignty by the United States, by right of exploration and the discovery of and entrance into the Columbia River by Captain Gray of the ship Columbia of Boston in the year 1792, was, however, finally settled by treaty with Spain in 1819.

To Captain Clarke is given the credit of being the first white man who trod Idaho's soil. In 1810 the Missouri Fur Company built Fort Henry, which was soon abandoned by that company. On Oct. 8, 1811, Wilson P. Hunt with a party of 60 men, being an overland expedition belonging to Astor's Pacific Fur Company, arrived at Fort Henry. Here detachments remained, to be sent out in the Rocky Mountains to trap, with the fort as a supply station and concentration with their furs. This may be considered as the first white settlement made in the Territory of Idaho. Hunt with his party proceeded on his way to the coast, moving down the Snake River, and after suffering great hardships, privations and perils arrived at Astoria, Feb. 15, 1812. This attempt to make a permanent occupation on the coast ended in disaster by the capture of Fort Astoria, Dec. 12, 1813, by a British armed vessel, the United States being then engaged in war with

Great Britain, and the name changed to Fort George. It was not until in the year 1818 that the fort was redelivered to an agent of the United States.

While it was generally believed that the Northwest was unfit for agricultural purposes, it was considered valuable for the furs which might be collected through trading with the natives and by trapping. After the disaster which befell the Pacific Fur Company it was not until the year 1823 that another effort was made to establish fur trading and trapping stations west of the Rocky Mountains. In that year W. H. Ashley crossed the mountains and returned to the States the same year; returning the following year to Green River, discovered Salt Lake, and erected a fort at Lake Ashley, where he left 100 men and returned to St. Louis. These successful ventures attracted others to a field so promising to the adventurous. In 1825 Jedediah S. Smith crossed the mountains with 40 men and passed into California. In 1829 Major Pilcher traveled down Clarke's Fork to Fort Colville, thence up the Columbia River to its source, and returned to the States. In 1832 Capt. B. L. E. Bonneville reached the Rocky Mountains; on Christmas, 1833, he started from camp, on Port Neuf River, on an expedition to Walla Walla. He reached Powder River Jan. 12, 1834; thence passed down Snake River, on the west, to Alpowa Creek; thence followed the old Nez Perce trail up stream across the Touchet and thence to Fort Walla Walla, where he arrived March 4, 1834. Two days after he started back with his Nez Perce guide and finally reached his camp of general rendezvous for his several expeditions. In the year 1835 he again started, with a formidable outfit, destined to the Willamette Valley, passing the Blue Mountains by way of the Grand Ronde Valley and the Umatilla River. In the year 1834 Nathaniel J. Wyeth of Boston led his second expedition with 60 men, crossed the Rocky Mountains, established Fort Hall, near the headwaters of Snake River, as an interior trading post, where he left 12 men and a stock of goods. This was undoubtedly the beginning of the first permanent white settlement in the limits of the present State of Idaho. Wyeth then passed down the Snake River and finally arrived at the mouth of the Willamette River, where he established Fort Williams. In the same year the Hudson Bay Company erected on Snake River, of poles, Fort Boise, but it was not occupied till the year 1835. This was afterward replaced by a more substantial structure of adobe.

This attempt to establish trading stations in the Northwest, like all preceding efforts, proved disastrous, financially, to the originators. The opposition of the powerful British Hudson Bay Company was too formidable to withstand, and the American posts were transferred to that company, Fort Hall passing into its possession also. This was the last effort made by American citizens to compete with that company for the native traffic.

Though such were the results, as business enterprises and the field of traffic was abandoned to British subjects, the territory was not wholly given over to British rule. Accompanying the Wyeth expedition were four self-sacrificing spirited men,—Rev. Jason Lee, Rev. Daniel Lee, Cyrus Shepard and P. L. Edwards,—who were sent out by the Methodist Missionary Board for the purpose of establishing a mission near the Columbia River. They selected a site, 60 miles above the mouth of the Willamette River, on which buildings were erected. It may be said that from the day of the arrival of the Wyeth expedition at its destination was begun the foundation of the future destiny and greatness of the Northwest. Hitherto those who ventured across the desolate and rugged pathway to the great ocean were those hardy spirits whose sole purposes were to reap the rewards of barter, the trap and the gun; whose thoughts were not to cultivate and beautify the desert and the wilderness. Being in search of immediate results, they were wanderers over the vast domain, and their attachments were regulated by the prospects of pecuniary profit. But with the advent of these missionaries, endowed with stubborn and aggressive wills for the right and with American hearts, they were destined to group about them a people whose independent principles would instill them to grapple with an arbitrary and powerful foreign corporation backed by English power. They came not for gain merely, but for the more holy and beneficent purposes of making homes and surrounding themselves with such comforts of civilization as a pioneer life would afford them, and to instruct the natives in the arts of agriculture and lead them in the paths of Christian duty, and over and above all should wave the Star-Spangled Banner of their country. Such were the class of pioneers, who could not fail to attract such emigrants from the States necessary to build up states in a territory where its people are savages and their country a desolate wilderness.

In 1836 there arrived at Fort Walla Walla Dr. Marcus Whitman and Rev. H. H. Spalding with their wives, and W. H. Gray, for the purpose of establishing missions under the auspices of the Presbyterian Board of Missions. They came overland with wagons, horses, mules, cattle and such necessary articles as they could transport. Doctor Whitman selected a site near Fort Walla Walla and erected mission buildings, where he, his wife and eleven other white persons were murdered by the Indians, November, 1847. Rev. H. H. Spalding selected a site in the country of the Nez Perces, in a beautiful valley on Lapwai Creek, 2 miles from its mouth and about 12 miles from Lewiston. With the aid of the Indians, buildings were erected and occupied about Dec. 20, 1836. This was the first mission established in Idaho. To this mission was brought and used the first printing press and material introduced in the Northwest territory. To the energy, patriotism and personal efforts of Doctor Whitman is due the defeat of the schemes of the Hudson Bay Company to secure all the territory north of the Columbia River to the sovereignty of England, and to attract the attention of the government and the American people to the value of the great territory which had been so long neglected because thought to be worthless. Accidentally becoming apprised of the purposes of that company, with but little preparation, he immediately started overland and reached the States in January, 1843. He was accorded interviews with President Tyler, Secretary of State Webster and members of Congress, in which he urged the importance of taking immediate action to extend the authority of the government over its territory, and save it from falling into the control of England. Surprised at the indifference of the heads of the government, who argued that the country was but barren deserts and rugged mountains,—unfit for agricultural purposes, to which emigration would never tend or seek, that it was not worth the expense of caring for,—Doctor Whitman labored to convince them of their erroneous ideas of the vast country, which had been industriously stimulated and encouraged by the Hudson Bay Company. To prove that their views were unfounded, he agreed to guide a train of emigrants to the coast. President Tyler promised to

await the result of the experiment before concluding, finally, the settlement of the boundary line. Starting from the rendezvous on the frontier, guided by Doctor Whitman, 875 persons, with their wagons loaded with the most necessary articles, and 1,300 head of cattle, reached the Columbia River in September, 1843.

The success of this expedition of emigrants to the Pacific Coast created a sentiment of enthusiasm which led to the treaty, signed June 15, 1846, establishing the boundary line, and the assumption by the National Government of its authority over all the territory south of the forty-ninth parallel. The tide of emigration thus begun, it continued with a steady but certain flow, so that by the census made in 1849 there were 9,083 persons in the territory.

In the year 1855 treaties were made with the Nez Perces and with the Flathead Nation, comprising the Flatheads, Kootenai and Pend d'Oreille tribes, by which those tribes relinquished all their lands except the reservations. These treaties by provisions therein were not obligatory upon either party until they were ratified by the President and Congress. As they were not ratified by the Senate until March 8, 1859, the country was not legally open to white settlement previous to the date of ratification. To this neglect on the part of the government may be attributed much of the causes which led to the outbreaks and depredations by the Indians in the years 1855 and 1856. The encroachments of the whites upon the territories of the Indians caused jealousies and suspicions on the part of the latter that the government was playing false with them by failing to perform the treaty agreements. In 1860 a party of miners from Walla Walla discovered gold in what afterward became the celebrated Oro Fino mining country. This was followed by a rush of emigration, and the discoveries of Rhodes' Creek, Elk Creek, Powder River and the Salmon River mines following in quick succession, the territory now comprising the State of Idaho became famous, and towns rapidly sprang up in the miner's wake.

In 1863 the first party of miners entered the Boise Basin. These were attacked by Shoshone and Bannock Indians and forced to retire. This led to sanguinary contests for supremacy. There was also a number of renegade Indians, who having been expelled from their tribes held no tribal relations, whose repeated depredations on the settlements led to their summary punishment in the winter of 1863. In 1877 occurred the trouble with the non-treaty Indians of the Nez Perce tribe under Chief Joseph, which ended with their capture and removal to Indian Territory. In 1878 and 1879 the Bannock and other tribes of lesser note in Southern Idaho began hostilities against the growing settlements, but they were captured by the troops after a short campaign and placed on reservations. Since 1879 there has been but little, if any, fears from Indians by the settlers. They have been placed on reservations and are, though slowly, acquiring habits tending toward civilization.

With the influx of mining experts and prospectors the great wealth which lay hidden in the mountains and valleys became known abroad, immigration soon demanded a territorial government, and the Territory of Idaho was created from parts of Washington, Dakota and Nebraska, by act of Congress passed March 13, 1863. In reorganizing the territories in 1868, Montana was wholly created out of Idaho and also a large part of Wyoming; Idaho retaining its present limits. As Idaho's unlimited mineral resources and the value of her agricultural lands became developed and known abroad, her population increased with a steady growth. Its people, realizing the importance of a state government, applied to Congress for admission to the Union. In pursuance to an act of Congress the people's representatives met in convention and submitted a constitution, which was ratified by the people at an election, and by proclamation of President Harrison Idaho was declared a state under the constitution of the United States.

IDAHO OFFICIALS.

Willis H. Pettit.
Geo. M. Parsons.
Joseph Pinkham.
Frank A. Fenn.

James F. Curtis.
Gov. Wm. J. McConnell.
Frank C. Ramsey.

Chas. S. Kingsley.
Wm. C. Hill.
B. Byron Lower.
Joseph Perrault.

PUBLIC BUILDINGS AT BOISE.
U S. Assay Office.   Public School.   State House

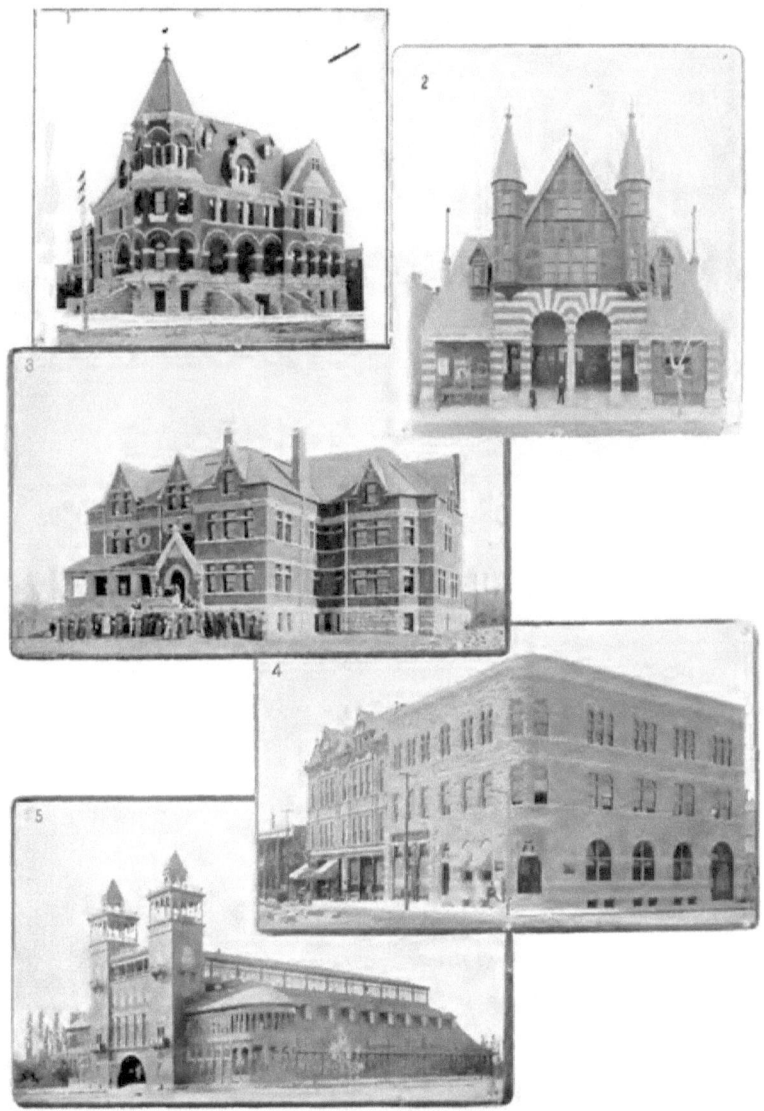

PUBLIC BUILDINGS AT BOISE.
No. 1—City Hall.   No. 2—Pinney's Opera House.   No. 3—St. Margaret's School.   No. 4—Boise National Bank and I. O. O. F. Blocks.
No. 5—Natatorium.

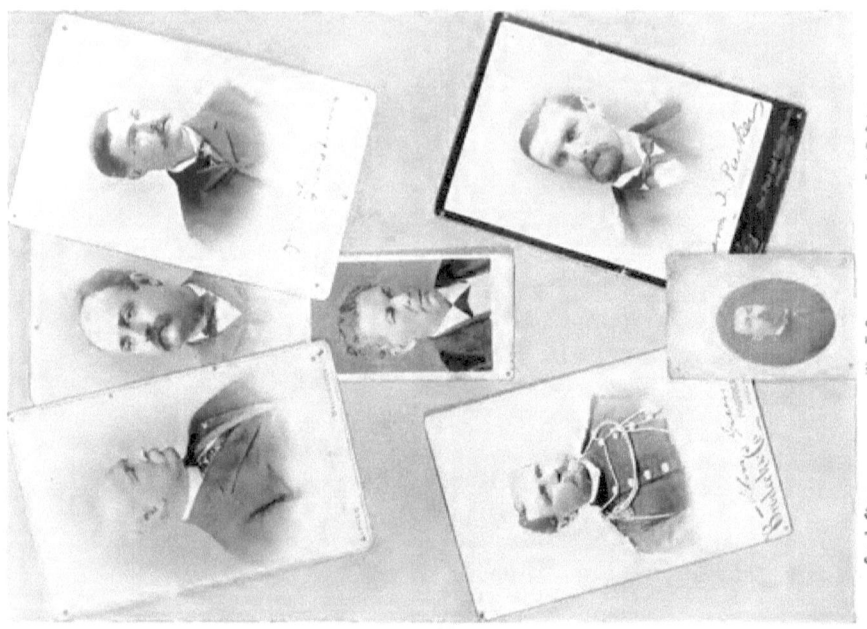

Fred. T. Dubois.
Aaron F. Parker.

Wm. T. Reeves.
Stephen A. Fenn.
James H. Hawley.

Geo. L. Shoup.
John Green.

THE WILLSON PLACER MINE.

DESCRIPTIVE.

THE State of Idaho comprises the territory lying between British Columbia on the north, the Territory of Utah and the State of Nevada on the south, the states of Montana and Wyoming on the east and the states of Oregon and Washington on the west. It extends about 410 miles north and south, with a width varying from 44 to 306 miles, containing 86,294 square miles, or 55,228,160 acres,—an area nearly as large as the states of New York and Pennsylvania. When Congress created it a territory, March 3, 1863, it embraced 325,000 square miles. By act passed May 25, 1868, creating the territories of Montana and Wyoming, Idaho was reduced to its present limits.

A bird's-eye view of the surface of the state would represent a wedge-shaped plateau with a rugged surface of valley, 700 feet above sea level in the extreme west, and hills and mountains attaining the height of 10,000 feet in the extreme east; and flowing among the craggy mountains, fertile hills and valleys, innumerable streams of clear, pure and cool water, rushing over rocks and precipices of great height, as if hastening to supply the thirsty lowlands, and then rushing onward to mingle its waters with those of the broad Pacific.

MOUNTAINS.

The word Idaho, given to the state, is an Indian word or term which interpreted signifies "Gem of the Mountains." This is literally true applied to Idaho. Under its rugged surface is hidden the richest minerals and valuable gems, awaiting the enterprise of man to utilize its wealth. Of the general surface of the state, a writer says: "Prof. F. V. Hayden, in his geological survey of the territories, in referring to the surface of a large portion of Idaho, describes it as literally crumpled or rolled up in one continuous series of mountain ranges, fold after fold. Perhaps even better examples of these remarkable folds may be found in the country drained by the Salmon River and its branches, where lofty ranges of mountains, for the most part covered with limestones and quartzites of the carboniferous age, wall in the little streams. None of our published maps convey any idea of the almost innumerable ranges. We might say that from longitude 110 degrees to 118 degrees, a distance of over 500 miles, there is a range of mountains on an average every 10 to 20 miles. Sometimes the distance across the range in a straight line, from the bed of a stream in one valley to the bed of the stream in the valley beyond the range, is not more than from 5 to 8 miles, while it is seldom more than 20 miles. From these statements," says the Professor, "which we believe to be correct, the reader may form some conception of the vast amount of labor yet to be performed to explore, analyze and locate on a suitable scale these hundreds of ranges of mountains, each one of which is worthy of a name."

If this should be considered an exaggerated description, it is nevertheless true that Idaho is a mountain state. Of the mountain ranges the Cœur d'Alene and the Bitter Root are in the north; part of the latter range with the crest of the Rocky and Wahsatch Mountains in the southeast form the east boundary of the state. The spurs from the ranges, especially the Rocky Mountains, are diffused well over the state. The Boise, Wood River, Salmon River and Sawtooth ranges occupy the central part, and the Owyhee in the southwest are the more prominent.

RIVERS.

With the exception of a few streams that flow from a small section in the southeast part of the state, which find their outlet in the great Salt Lake Basin, the rivers of Idaho contribute their waters to swell the great Columbia. Idaho can enumerate its rivers by scores. The most important are the Snake, Clearwater, Spokane and Pend d'Oreille. The sources of the Snake are near those of the Yellowstone in the Rocky Mountains in Wyoming, at an elevation of 8,000 feet. Entering Idaho, gathering the waters of its numerous tributaries, its torrents flow southwardly about 500 miles, sweeping westerly, with a graceful bend to the south turns northwardly, masking the westerly limits of the state, until it reaches Lewiston, thus describing, roughly, a great arc of a circle. Thence it swerves westerly into the State of Washington, and sweeps onward in its majestic course to deposit its waters into the Columbia.

The volume of water held and discharged by the Snake is enormous; in places the depths are so great that soundings to the depth of 240 feet and more have failed to reach bottom. It is navigable 150 miles above its junction with Clarke's Fork, which was the original for the Columbia north of Snake River. Its total length is nearly 1,000 miles.

The Salmon, Weiser, Payette, Boise and Wood rivers, which drain the central and southern part of the state, flow into the Snake River from the north. Entering Snake River from the south, and draining the great county of Owyhee, are the Bruneau and the Owyhee rivers.

In the north are the Clearwater, which empties into the Snake at Lewiston, and Cœur d'Alene, which flows into the lake of that name. The Spokane, which is the outlet of Lake Cœur d'Alene, passes into the State of Washington and enters the Columbia. Clarke's Fork, flowing into Idaho from the Rocky Mountains in Montana, empties into Pend d'Oreille Lake and thence, under the name of Pend d'Oreille River, empties into the Columbia River; and the Cœur d'Alene and St. Joseph rivers empty into Lake Cœur d'Alene. The Kootenai is also an important stream tributary to the Columbia.

Mountainous regions are noted for their numerous springs, which is also true of Idaho. From the foothills to the mountains everywhere flows springs of water clear as crystal and ice-cold or warm and hot, which are the sources of the streams which supply the greater rivers. Many of these springs send forth immense volumes of water and supply the cities and towns with an abundance of pure water. South from Mountain Home may be seen one of the wonderful springs which has burst from the palisades of the Snake, and a river of water plunges with terrific force into the torrents below, a depth of several hundred feet. Many springs possess valuable medicinal qualities, and are sought with much favor by invalids.

VALLEYS.

It is estimated that within the state there are 13,000 square miles of valley land situated at an elevation of less than 3,000 feet, 10,000 between 3,000 and 4,000, 22,000 between 4,000 and 5,000 and 19,000 square miles between 5,000 and 6,000 feet.

Robert E. Strathorn, Esq., prepared the following list of the prominent valleys, with their length and breadth:

NAME AND LOCATION OF VALLEY.	LENGTH. Miles.	BREADTH. Miles.
South Fork of Snake River, Eastern Idaho	50	2 to 4
Salt River Valley, Eastern Idaho	30	2 to 2
Bear River Valley, Eastern Idaho	40	3 to 5
Snake Valley, North Fork, Eastern Idaho	60	3 to 10
Blackfoot Valley, Eastern Idaho	70	2 to 5
Round Valley, Eastern Idaho	50	8 to 12
Wood River Valley, Central Idaho	90	1 to 2
Camas Prairie, Central Idaho	60	15 to 25
Boise Valley, Western Idaho	60	2 to 6
Payette Valley, Western Idaho	75	2 to 15
Weiser Valley, Western Idaho	40	2 to 5
Lemhi Valley, Northeastern Idaho	70	3 to 6
Palansani Valley, Northeastern Idaho	25	1 to 5
Northern Camas Prairie, North Idaho	30	10 to 25
Potlatch Valley, North Idaho	25	10 to 15
Palouse Valley, North Idaho	60	5 to 10
St. Joseph Valley, North Idaho	45	5 to 10

The above list does not include all the valleys in the state; there are numerous others, where pleasant homes in beautiful vales, nestled in the hills, where settlers can establish ranches for grazing sheep, horses and cattle, or for farming purposes. The soil of the valleys is surprisingly rich in power to promote vegetation, and is capable of producing large crops for an indefinite time without fertilizers.

LAKES.

Nearly every county in Idaho has its lake with its placid waters surrounded with Nature's parks. Lakes of every description abound in the mountain ranges.

Kootenai County can boast of some of the finest lakes and picturesque scenery in the world. In her territory rests Cœur d'Alene, Pend d'Oreille, Kanisku, Cocolalla and numerous smaller lakes. Cœur d'Alene Lake is about 30 miles long and a varying width from 2 to 4 miles. A line of steamers ply regularly from Cœur d'Alene City to the old mission. Its waters are clear and cool and abound in fish. The banks are mountainous, covered with timber. The Cœur d'Alene Indian Reservation surrounds it on the north, west and south. The Cœur d'Alene, St. Joseph and St. Mary's rivers flow into it, and the Spokane is the outlet.

Lake Pend d'Oreille is about 60 miles in length and a width varying from 3 to 15 miles. Though classed as a lake, it is, in fact, but a broadening of the Clarke's Fork, whose rushing waters sweep down from its mountain gorges to find a pathway along the verdure-clad mountains, which present an enchanting panorama that strikes the visitor with awe, wonder and admiration. A trestle 8,400 feet in length crosses a neck of the lake, on which the Northern Pacific trains pass, from the car windows of which fine views of the unsurpassed natural scenery may be obtained.

Kanisku Lake, in the northern part of the county, is about 20 miles long and 10 miles wide, and is located in a region hitherto unexplored. The recent construction of the Great Northern Railway has created an interest in Northern Idaho which must result in settlements and further development of that region.

The people of Lewiston find a charming resort in Lake Waha. Though small, it is sought for pleasure and pastime, which is greatly enhanced by its abundance of fish. An entranced writer says of it: "Nothing we have ever seen can exceed the tranquil beauty of this sylvan, this idyllic scene, with its mountain solitudes unbroken by discordant sound, and its wealth of charming landscapes and xanthic skies."

Payette Lake, the source of the Payette River, situated in Boise County, is a favorite resort for the people of Boise City and neighborhood. Surrounded by mountains, it is 10 miles long and 5 miles in width, and is particularly noted for its trout, redfish and whitefish. It is of unknown depth. Soundings of 2,600 feet have failed to reach the bottom.

So numerous are the lakes in Idaho that more space than can be allotted to this work would be required. Many of them are noted for their picturesque landscape and beauty.

CLIMATE.

It is well known that high altitudes affect the temperature and to a certain degree lower elevations. Therefore, that the mountain ranges and their ramifications over the State of Idaho make it a cold and inhospitable climate, is believed by those who have not become familiar with the peculiar conditions which operate to give Idaho a climate, taken altogether, one of the finest in the world, where health is marked higher than any other state in the Nation. As the State of Idaho is in the same latitude as France, Switzerland, Spain and Portugal, it is subject to oceanic influences similar to those which are exerted on the Atlantic Coast of Europe and the British Isles. As the Gulf Stream crossing the Atlantic, carrying its heated waters and diffusing its warmth to those countries, so, in like manner, are the lands adjacent to the Pacific Ocean warmed by the great Japan current (Kuro Siva). This mighty stream bearing directly against the American shores warms the atmosphere passing over it, and the genial balmy Chinook winds carry their modifying influence far inland, even into Montana.

To emphasize these facts, follow the isothermal lines which mark the northern limit of wheat production. Starting near the mouth of the St. Lawrence River, at latitude 50 degrees, thence running in a northwesterly direction across the continent, when directly north of Idaho it will be found that the northern limit has increased and is nearly 1,000 miles north of the extreme northern boundary of this state, the cause of which is the influence of the current as stated. A few comparisons may be pertinent to further illustrate the isothermal difference between the temperature east of the Rocky Mountains and that on the west side. The average mean temperature in Northern Idaho is 56 degrees, a milder showing by 5 degrees than is made by Ohio, milder by 10 degrees than Iowa, and milder by 12 degrees than Maine and New Hampshire. Boise City, in Western Central Idaho, with an altitude much greater than Lewiston, being 2,800 feet, has an average temperature of 51 degrees, the same as Ohio, and 4 degrees warmer than Connecticut. The rain and snow fall at Lewiston is about 24 inches; at Boise City it is about 12. At the latter place the lowest record during seven consecutive winters was 12 degrees below zero in the month of January, and the highest 108 degrees in July. The United States Signal Office reports that the mercury sank below zero only four times during one period of five years. The prevailing winds are south-southwest, averaging 12 miles an hour, the greatest velocity not exceeding 30.

Boise City has been selected as a fair representative of the average temperature of the agricultural sections. The more elevated mining districts have a lower temperature, with a greater snowfall and as harsh winters as are experienced in the Alleghany or Blue Ridge Mountains. But the best authorities on climatology agree that in the dry, rarefied atmosphere of Idaho and the mountainous regions on the east there is a difference of 20 degrees in the intensity of heat and cold in favor of those regions, when compared with the raw and humid atmosphere of the Atlantic Coast; so that a temperature of 100 degrees in Idaho is only equal in effects upon the system to one of 85 degrees in Boston or New York, or the extreme cold temperature at Boise of 12 degrees below zero is endured as that of 8 degrees above at any point in the Eastern States. Hon. E. A. Stevenson, late governor of the territory, referring to this peculiarity of its climate, says: "The lowest temperature in the history of the Boise Signal Station was —27.8 degrees, on Jan. 16, 1888. At this time the signal officer regularly walked from his office to his residence and back without an overcoat, and he noticed many other men on the streets without overcoats. Such habits are very possible in the exceptionally fine climate of Idaho. This occurred during the twenty days when 1,000 persons froze to death between the Rocky Mountains and the Mississippi River. Rarely ever does the temperature fall to zero. This highly oxygenated atmosphere is specially adapted to the cure of catarrh, consumption and many diseases in which a cure depends upon a purification of the blood. At this date (October 9th) there has been no frost. The most tender vines and flowers are as vigorous and fresh as in the spring."

Open-air work is performed every day in the year; sunstroke and hydrophobia are unknown in the state. The population who live on the mines and in the stock ranges and are predominant in numbers will shelter in the rudest and most fragile constructions the year round, and a case of freezing rarely if ever occurs.

Cloudy days are an exception and the clear sunshine is the rule. Idaho averages 260 clear days free from clouds and shows 300 fair days against 191 fair days in Boston, 170 at Buffalo and Chicago. Of 600 cyclones reported by the United States Signal Service during five years, not one occurred in Idaho. Floods and storms are unknown in the state. Rarely does rain fall during harvest time, and the absence of showers is not felt, because of the beneficial distribution of lands and streams suitable for irrigation; hence loss of crops by disastrous floods or droughts would be considered phenomenal. The snowfall in the valleys is light, rarely enough for sleighing in many parts of the state.

HEALTH.

From the statement of the average temperature it will be seen that Idaho compares favorably with her sister states in the matter of climate; but with her peculiar conformation, her location and geological formation, the influence which they exert from a sanitary point, Idaho stands pre-eminent. Vital statistics show that Idaho has no equal in the United States, and probably none elsewhere. The statistics of mortality in the United States, collected by the Census Bureau, confirm this statement, as will be seen from the following table, which gives the exact figures from the census report:

Idaho	0.33
Alabama	1.06
Arizona	2.61
Arkansas	1.96
California	1.61
Florida	1.71
Georgia	1.18
Illinois	1.33
Indiana	1.05
Iowa	0.81
Kansas	1.25
Kentucky	1.09
Louisiana	2.06
Maine	1.73
Maryland	1.71
Massachusetts	1.77
Michigan	0.94
Minnesota	0.80
Mississippi	1.11
Missouri	1.85
Montana	0.90
New Hampshire	1.35
New Jersey	1.17
New Mexico	1.28
Colorado	0.91
Connecticut	1.96
Dakota	0.71
Delaware	1.75
District of Columbia	1.33
New York	1.98
Nebraska	0.81
Nevada	1.45
North Carolina	0.98
Ohio	1.11
Oregon	0.69
Pennsylvania	1.49
Rhode Island	1.86
South Carolina	1.05
Tennessee	1.13
Texas	1.37
Utah	1.05
Vermont	1.02
Virginia	1.24
Washington	0.93
West Virginia	0.91
Wisconsin	0.91
Wyoming	0.81

Scan the figures which the table presents. Florida, California and Colorado, states endowed with genial climates which approach perpetual spring and summer, the favorite resorts whence tens of thousands, seeking a renewal of their impaired health, flee in the hope of restoration; where the most eminent of the medical profession in the Eastern States unite in directing multitudes for the same purpose, present an unfavorable comparison with the health-restoring climate of Idaho. Florida shows a mortality nearly three times greater than Idaho, California nearly five times greater and Colorado nearly three times greater.

Again, refer to the following tables of the mortality of the United States Army at the several military stations distributed over the country. It is well known that the troops in the army are subjected to the same conditions and surroundings, and have the same habits in like proportions everywhere, more than any other class of people. Wherever their place of abode and whatever the climate, their food, clothing and medical attendance are identically the same. A comparison of mortality of persons under such similarity of conditions is of a higher value in estimating the actual healthfulness of each region than that obtained in the usual manner.

The percentages of death from disease to each 1,000 soldiers in the different military districts of the United States as reported by the Surgeon General, the average of many years, are:

LOCALITIES.	DEATHS EACH YEAR FROM DISEASE.
Gulf States	12.50
Atlantic Coast States	17.83
Arizona	12.11
Pennsylvania and Michigan	6.05
New Mexico	7.27
Montana	5.62
California	6.33
Dakota	4.70
Wyoming	4.71
Idaho	3.71

During the years 1868 and 1869 the number of cases of sickness (not death) by malarial fever occurring in an equal number of soldiers in the different departments show the following proportions:

Department of the East	30
Department of the South	60
Department of the Lakes	50
New Mexico, Indian Territory, Kansas, Arkansas and Missouri, over	40
Wyoming, Nebraska and Utah	30
Montana, Dakota and Minnesota, nearly	30
Department of the Columbia (Oregon, Washington and Idaho)	30
Department of California	30
Department of Arizona	100

Continuing, we may select the mortality occasioned by the great destroyers of human life, consumption and other respiratory diseases. In every 1,000 soldiers there die annually of consumption, pneumonia, etc.:

In Florida	2.75
Texas	3
New Mexico	3.15
California, a little more than	3
IDAHO, ONLY	1.6

From these statistics, one taken from the inhabitants generally throughout the state, and the other from the military in their respective departments, it is conclusively shown that the State of Idaho stands first and is the very healthiest part of the United States.

We may go further, and Idaho will bear comparison with the most healthful favored country in the world. Italy, Southern France and Algiers, to which invalids are sent, both civil and military statistics show a much higher mortality than Idaho. In presenting the figures on the subject treated fairness has been observed. Particular years have been selected, not that they favor a theory, but because they are obtainable and are in form to be compared. During the years from 1860 to 1876 the death rate per annum from all diseases in the Italian Army was about 11 in each 1,000; among the French Army stationed in the south of France in 1872 it was 10 in 1,000; in the French Army in Algiers during the years 1863-64-66-70 it was 14 50. Comparing these with the death rate in Idaho from 1868 to 1881, which was only 3.75 in 1,000 by all diseases, the latter is healthier than the most highly extolled sections of Europe.

Of diseases of the respiratory organs, including consumption, pneumonia, etc., we have among the soldiers in the south of France (including the health resorts of Nice, Mentone, etc.), for the year 1872, an average death rate by these diseases of 2.4 per 1,000 annually. In the French Army in Algiers during the years 1863-64-66 it was by these diseases more than 3 in 1,000 annually. In the Italian Army during the years 1867-68-69-74-75-76 the deaths by these same diseases (consumption, etc.) averaged nearly 4 in 1,000, while in Idaho the mortality by these diseases from 1876 to 1881 was less than 1 in 1,000 annually— still maintaining her position as the most healthful locality.

Continuing the examination of mortality statistics, it is found that the records of the British medical departments do not detract, but confirm, the claim that Idaho has the healthiest country in the world. English soldiers are distributed all over the world, and the record represents the healthfulness and the unhealthfulness of climate in portions of all quarters of the globe. So that the British official military records are especially valuable.

At the British station of Gibraltar, the Ionian Islands and Malta, in the sanitary zone of the Mediterranean, the average death rate by all diseases during the years from 1859 to 1879 was about 7.5, 8.4 and 10.5 respectively in each 1,000 troops per annum ; and by respiratory diseases, including consumption, pneumonia, etc., of 2 in 1,000, being more than twice as great as in Idaho. In Australia the deaths by all diseases were 12 in each 1,000 troops annually, and by respiratory diseases 5 in 1,000. In New Zealand, of 8.75 by all diseases and nearly 3 per 1,000 by respiratory diseases. These are exceeded greatly in Japan, China and the East Indies, having a mortality from 14 to 25 in each 1,000 troops. In the West Indies, by all diseases, from 10 to 12 and 13 in 1,000, and respiratory diseases over 2 per annum. In England the mortality is about 8 in 1,000 from all diseases, and from respiratory diseases over 3.5. Coming into Canada it is between 6 and 7 per 1,000 by all diseases, and 2 by respiratory diseases. Continuing west into British Columbia, north and adjoining Idaho, where the climate is similar to that of Northern Idaho, the death rate per annum for the four and a half years the British troops were there was a little over 3 in 1,000 by all diseases, being almost the same as among the soldiers in Idaho in the Department of the Columbia.

The reader, after examining the recorded facts and experiences from all quarters of the globe, must arrive at the conviction that Idaho, and the adjacent territory extending from the Rocky Mountains to the Pacific Coast, is the *healthiest region in the world,* so far as positive and reliable evidence shows.

TIMBER.

The traveler who for the first time enters Idaho and crosses the state by way of the Union Pacific Railway, is unfavorably impressed, after traveling the monotonous sage plains which stretch out far to the right and to the left, little dreaming that beyond in the north begins a region covered with timber that, the further it is penetrated the greater is the wonder and admiration experienced by the beholder. The forest area of Idaho is computed to contain 7,000,000 acres. Throughout the central, northern and eastern part of the state the timber lands possess a growth much heavier than in the timbered states of the East, while in the remaining sections the timber supply is equal to that of most of the prairie states.

From careful estimates from eighteen different parts of the state, from *data* furnished by Messrs. Williams and Paul, statisticians, and from Doctor Brewster's "Forests of America," the area of these woodlands may be, approximately, safely placed as follows : Ten thousand square miles contain over 500 acres of timber to the square mile ; 12,000 square miles from 360 to 500 acres ; 5,000 square miles from 250 to 360 acres ; 15,000 square miles from 120 to 240 acres ; 13,500 square miles from 10 to 120 acres. Leaving the treeless plains in Southern Idaho, extensive timber forests will be found in Boise, Lemhi, Custer and Alturas counties. It is estimated that the amount of merchantable timber in the region of the upper waters of the Boise River, its tributaries, excluding the South Fork, will reach from 80,000,000 to 90,000,000 feet. It is claimed by experts that the South Fork is much more heavily timbered than the above estimated section of the Boise. These forests extend 30 or 40 miles into the mountains, and abound in fir, white pine and cottonwood. The same timber is found in abundance on the tributaries of the Upper Salmon River.

In Idaho County, on the Salmon and Craig's Mountains, is found an extensive body of timber extending to Snake River near the mouth of Salmon River and across the Clearwater, about 60 miles. This belt of timber is from 5 to 10 miles wide, and consists in part of white and yellow pine, red and yellow fir and white cedar. This body of timber is of large growth and valuable for lumbering purposes. Spruce and tamarack are found on Lolo Creek. Yew trees a foot in diameter are found on the upper part of the Clearwater. White pine logs 10 feet in diameter and 100 feet in length have been rafted down the Clearwater, furnishing the finest quality of lumber for finishing purposes.

Shoshone and Kootenai counties, in the extreme northern part of the state, are heavily timbered. Cœur d'Alene County also possesses fine woodland with much valuable timber. The Pend d'Oreille forests extend in all directions from the lake, covering an area over 100 miles square. In these forests stand huge monarchs, whose tops reach the height of 200 feet; the bull pine, white pine, tamarack and fir predominating; while the cedar attains marvelous heights and thickness. The Spanish moss is seen hanging in long, graceful festoons from many of the trees, adding variety to the somber scene. "This superb forest of the Pend d'Oreille," observes a writer in the *Century Magazine,* "is a vast lumber preserve for future generations. The pineries of Michigan and Minnesota look like open parks compared with it. Nowhere else in the United States, save on the western slopes of the western mountains in Washington, can be found such a prodigious amount of timber to the acre.

The products of the Payette forests, which are among the finest in Central Idaho, find ready market along the Union Pacific Railway, and furnish a supply to the demand for building and other purposes all over Southern Idaho.

SOIL.

The soils of Idaho are much of the same general nature as those which are found in all the volcanic regions of the Northwest. They are composed of decayed, volcanic matter and the disintegration, through ages, of lava, basaltic and other rocks, which form the richest producing soil, and the most enduring under cultivation in the world. Soils vary according to location, and in Idaho are of four classes:

First — The mountain soil, especially in the timbered sections, is exceedingly rich in vegetable mould, and is deep and black.

Second — Plains and plateau soils contain all the elements required for the production of vegetation. It is estimated that three-fourths of the arable lands of Idaho are of this class.

Third — The valley soils are of the highest excellence. They consist of the accumulations on the sides of the mountains of decaying vegetable matter for unknown ages, and will produce, unsurpassed, all products which are adapted to the climate of the state.

Fourth — An alkali soil which is superabundant in a soluble salt, deleterious to most kinds of vegetation. The lands with this soil are limited in extent. Its natural products are greasewood and salt grass, which are readily eaten by cattle. Deep plowing and leaching by irrigation will in time free the soil of much of the injurious salts, when it will be found to be highly fertile, producing fine crops of the cereals.

The best results from any of these soils where destitute of a sufficiency of moisture cannot be had without the application of water either by rainfall or by irrigation. In many sections surprisingly large crops are obtained without irrigation, the soil being adapted to retain the moisture absorbed from the slight rainfall, snows and atmosphere, and generously supplying it to the growing vegetation. The dreary sagebush plains, touched with the life-giving waters from the springs and mountain streams, give astonishing evidence of the vegetative powers which have long awaited the advent of civilized enterprise. And it is for man to lead the crystal waters from the lakes and streams to feed the thirsty soil by means of irrigation, and receive his reward in the rich returns of wonderful crops of grains, fruits, vegetables, in fact all vegetation adapted to the climate.

THE IDAHO LEGISLATURE.

1 Lieut. Gov. F. B. Willis.	15 T. W. Girton.	29 F. W. Hunt.	43 J. Morris Howe.
2 Speaker D. T. Miller.	16 John S. Barrett.	30 John G. Brown.	44 Green White.
3 James H. McPherson.	17 John D. Benson.	31 F. C. Moss.	45 Henry F. Johnson
4 Norman M. Ruick.	18 Alex. Robertson.	32 George H. Stewart.	46 Hugh F. McCarter.
5 John L. Underwood.	19 P. Gaffney.	33 G. F. Fletcher.	47 Robert Neill.
6 Henry H. Bangs.	20 George J. Lewis.	34 Ralph A. Cowden.	48 James J. Story.
7 John I. Mitcham.	21 J. G. Watts.	35 Alex. Mayhew.	49 L. E. Workman.
8 Wm. J. Bogard.	22 Robert Campbell.	36 E. J. Turner.	50 A. A. Crane.
9 Swan A. Anderson.	23 C. G. Cartmell	37 Fred L. Burgen.	51 D. S. Mahana.
10 H. H. Clay.	24 J. Merrill.	38 William Allison.	52 F. J. Mills
11 J. E. Miller.	25 Walter Clevinger.	39 John F. Affington.	53 Andrew J. Hopper.
12 B. F. Morris	26 Wm. R. King	40 Paul P. Lawson	54 D. C. Stephens.
13 J. W. Ballentine	27 James J. McCarthy.	41 Charles Heam.	55 F. S. Yearian.
14 Rufus A. Caldwell.	28 E. S. Suydam.	42 John C. Greaves.	

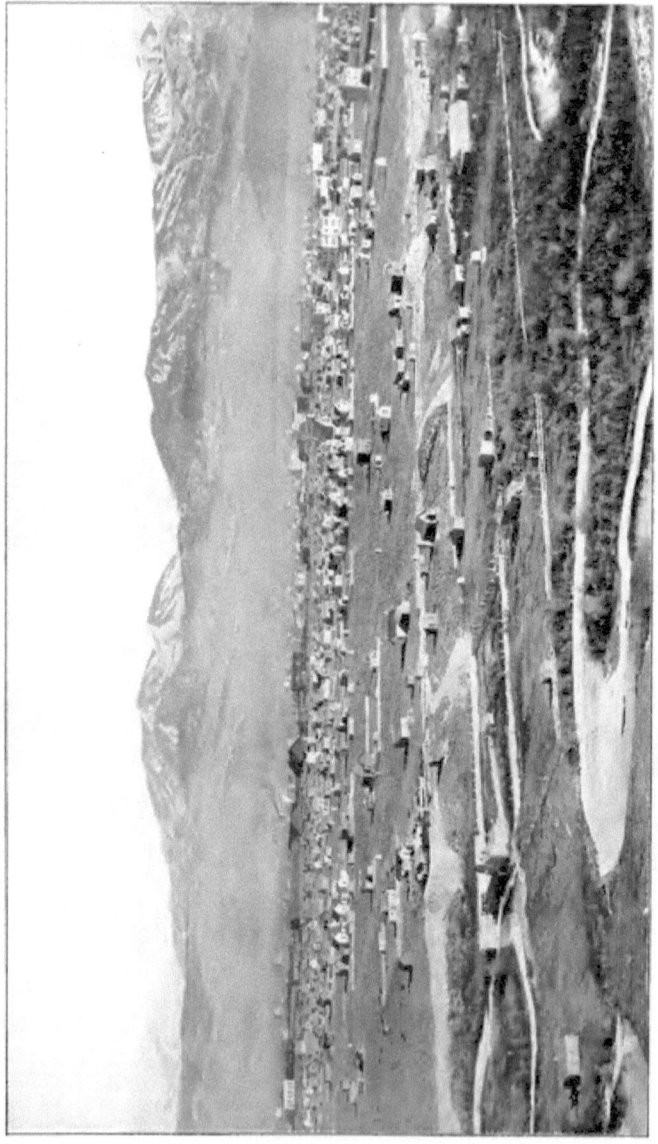

CITY OF POCATELLO.

IDAHO—THE GEM OF THE MOUNTAINS.

AGRICULTURE IN IDAHO.

The mining interest is predominant in the state, and the cultivation of the soil has kept well up to the requirements of the demand. It is expected that there will be a continued increase of the demand for the products of the soil. Many sections are capable, as stated, of producing large crops without irrigation; and the great wheat and other grain belts in the state are now so produced.

It is estimated that there are from 12,000,000 to 15,000,000 acres of valley and upland which can be irrigated and made productive. The process of irrigation is by means of canals or channels to conduct the water from streams and springs and distribute it through the lands intended for cultivation. It is the mode adopted more than 3,000 years ago by the ancient Egyptians in the valley of the Nile.

The cost of clearing the sagebrush and digging the ditches is from fifty cents to $1.25 per acre, being much less than the cost of clearing the timber land in the East. Canal companies that have irrigating canals charge from seventy-five cents to $1.25 per acre per year, or they will sell perpetual rights, subject to assessments for repairs, at from $6 to $8 per acre. In some locations committees may unite and construct canals for their own benefit.

Irrigation is more or less necessary in Southern and Central Idaho. In Northern Idaho, where there is greater rainfall, it is resorted to in occasional cases only. A brief statement of some of the principal farming productions in Idaho must suffice to attract attention to the merits of Idaho.

Wheat—All varieties, both spring and fall, of this staple are grown at all altitudes. The average yield is placed at 30 bushels. Fields sometimes yield 60, and many have produced 80 bushels per acre. The quality of Idaho wheat is not excelled, the berry being plump, hard and bright, and is rarely affected by the evils common to the crops in many regions.

Barley—Of this grain the same may be said as of wheat, except that the yield per acre averages 40 bushels, a single crop often exceeding 80 bushels per acre.

Oats—Growing everywhere, the yield is from 55 to 75 bushels, usually weighing 45 pounds to the bushel.

Rye—In every section of the state the finest quality of rye is raised. It is sown in the spring and the fall and largely used for pasture.

Flax—In some parts of Northern Idaho considerable attention is paid to the cultivation of flax. It produces from 20 to 30 bushels per acre.

Corn—The nights are too cool to produce good crops in the state. Yet there is grain of excellent quality raised, particularly in some of the lower valleys, as Boise, Payette and Weiser.

Broom Corn and Sorghum—Are successfully cultivated. The latter is especially rich in the sweet juice.

Tobacco and Sweet Potatoes—Are successfully grown in milder belts of the state.

Grasses—As the natural grasses abound, less attention has been given to the tame varieties. The blue grass, orchard grass, red top, timothy, alfalfa and clover have each been successfully grown in the localities to which they are adapted. Alfalfa is especially adapted to all sections and is the favorite for general cultivation; its yield being so great that credibility is severely taxed to realize its truth. Its fattening and dairy qualities are superior to all others.

Fruits—Practical experience has demonstrated that apples, peaches, pears, apricots, nectarines, plums, grapes, etc., also the various small fruits, are adapted to and thrive in Idaho. They yield large crops, the fruit growing to great size and of superior flavor.

Vegetables—Potatoes of very excellent quality yield large crops, and large shipments have been made to Eastern markets. All kinds of vegetables, as beets, peas, squashes, beans, tomatoes, cucumbers, onions, etc., are cultivated with success, yielding large crops of good quality and prodigious size.

WHEAT AND STOCK RAISING.

Wheat.

That the production of wheat in Idaho absorbs the chief attention of the farming community is not surprising when attention is directed to the ease which attends its cultivation, the harvesting and the large yield per acre, compared to the labor and expense required in its production in the Eastern States. The improved modes in cultivation and the improvements in all kinds of farm implements have stimulated the farmer to increase his production by cultivating more land at less cost than formerly. This stimulation has tended to produce increased crops from constantly increasing cultivated acres, more rapid than the increase of population demanded. Thus an overproduction has followed with correspondingly low prices. This depression of price must at an early date result in reducing the area in those Eastern states which are rapidly assuming high rank as manufacturing centres. The great cost in producing a bushel of wheat in those sections will tend to reduce the aggregate crop, and with a like cost they cannot successfully compete with the wheat-growing regions of the Northwest, which is emphatically a natural wheat belt and will always in the future hold rank above competition for successful production. As the cultivated area of the best wheat-producing lands in the United States is reaching its limit, with the population increasing toward the point of consumption, so will the product advance in value.

The wheat lands of Idaho, by reason of their everlasting fertility and their large return to the cultivator, are especially commended to the wheat grower or farmer. A visit to some of the large grain fields in Idaho during harvest excites wonder when one sees the broad acres of golden grain falling under the harvest sickle, then carried to the thresher, and, in an incredibly short time, sees the grain, which a few moments before was standing in the field, sacked ready for shipping to a distant market.

There are in Idaho 16,000,000 acres of land classed as agricultural, of which about two-thirds require irrigation. These lie principally in Southern Idaho. Under a system of irrigation, the husbandman who has once cultivated his land with the assistance of irrigated water will pronounce it more satisfactory in its results than when compelled to trust to the fickleness of the clouds, which may bring a sufficiency, a superabundance to destroy, or abandon them to burning droughts. The advantage is with the farmer, when at his will his crops are revived with refreshing supplies of water and repay his attention with generous crops ranging from 30 to 80 bushels per acre. Those sections which are cultivated without irrigation are chiefly in the northern part of the state, in the rich valleys and in the mountain slopes. The total yield in the wheat belt is, in the aggregate, very large, and increases each year. In this region is included the wonderful fertile valleys of the Potlatch, Genesee, Paradise, North Palouse, all noted for their surprising wheat production, as high as 80 bushels machine measure having been produced per acre. Such yields are probably exceptional, however, but to show that they average largely, compare the average yield of Idaho with the states named in the following table showing the production per acre of the staples named:

	WHEAT.	RYE.	OATS.	BARLEY.	POTATOES.	CORN.
Idaho	30	15	55	40	250	15
Nevada	19	...	31	...	95	30
California	12	15	30	23	112	31
Oregon	21	14	31	25	95	35
Eastern States	13	15	31	25	69	26

It will be seen that Idaho leads the highest producing section 9 bushels and the Eastern States 17 bushels per acre. Cannot Idaho honestly and truthfully present her claims to agriculturists seeking new homes for grain growing?

Now, in case the reader thinks of locating or investing in an agricultural region, why not visit Idaho and investigate the most profitable wheat-raising section?

IDAHO=THE GEM OF THE MOUNTAINS.

Stock Raising.

With 25,000,000 acres of grazing lands covered with indigenous grasses highly nutritious in all of the qualities requisite for grazing purposes, Idaho presents special inducements to the stock growers. Botanists who have investigated the native grasses growing in the state say that there are thirteen different kinds, hardy and vigorous to withstand the severest rigors of the climate, that are valuable for grazing purposes. Chief and most abounding is the bunch grass, so named from its growing in bunches from a stool similar to timothy grass. There are several varieties, two of which are most popular. It is probable that location may have caused the diversity, as the lower bench lands next to the bottom are the home of one variety, and the higher rolling hills and mountains are the favorite haunts of another. These are considered about equal in value; but the former is thought best for cattle and the latter for sheep—a kind provision in Nature, as the rolling hills and mountains are also better adapted to that animal.

When the snow has been heavy during the winter and the ground well moistened, or there has been heavy rains or snow in the spring, the grass starts early and the growth may be expected to be heavy. It ripens in the latter part of June. If there should be an exceptional season it may remain green till September. However, the standing growth has been cured, retaining its elements of nutrition, which all kinds of stock devour ravenously. Stock raising in Idaho is not an experiment. It has proven a success, as evidenced by the number now owned in the state. There are of cattle over 400,000; of horses, 140,000. The favorite mode of grazing is to pasture on the mountains in summer and remove the herds to lower elevations where shelter from inclement weather and food can be had should it be required. In the range stock business, the herds of cattle and bands of horses are left to range freely over the mountains and hills at will. In most parts of the state horses and cattle will winter without hay or grain, thriving on bunch or other native grasses, the sweet sage, etc. The stockman who exercises vigilance, care in the management of his stock, keeping them together that they may not wander into other herds, attention to branding, seeing that they have food in reserve in case of an emergency arising from an unusual inclement season, will certainly succeed in the business. The old breeds of horses and cattle are being replaced with better grades. Thoroughbreds and high grades of all the most approved breeds have been introduced in the state, and fine animals are seen in most ranges.

There is wealth in stock raising under judicious management. Twenty-five years ago large sums of money were invested in range cattle on the plains of Nebraska, Kansas, Montana and other states east of the Rocky Mountains. Capitalists who knew little or nothing of the practical management required in stock ranging, invested largely in cattle, hoping to increase their wealth from the open and untaxed lands of the plains and mountains. The stimulation thus given to the business increased the numbers enormously, producing great competition, which resulted in large losses. This, with the settlers crowding the range held by the large ranches, is placing in the hands of the farmer opportunities to compete with the latter on a smaller though profitable scale. It requires a larger capital to embark in raising horses than it does cattle. A farmer moving on a ranch near a range with a few cows can in a few years gather about him a fine herd of grazing cattle. In whatever section one may go he will find farmers who have become wealthy from stock raising, and that the business is not overtaxed with competition. The extension of railroad systems will develop the country and afford quick transportation to the best market points.

There are in Idaho over 400,000 sheep. The mountains and hills are eminently adapted to the raising of these useful animals. These elevated ranges are the natural home of the sheep, where the diseases to which they are subject on the lowlands seldom come, and they thrive and withstand an unusually vigorous climate. Sheep raising is the poor man's opportunity in Idaho, as it is claimed that no other branch of stock raising will bring wealth and independence so quickly as sheep raising on a small capital.

As with all other undertakings, some knowledge and experience, in combination with proper care and attention to their wants and safety, are requisite to success. Sheep thrive on the scantiest pastures when necessary and endure the lowest temperature with moderate feed. Beginning with a band containing 100 sheep, in the course of a decade it will increase to a number incredible to those unacquainted with the profits of sheep raising. A small capital will suffice a poor man to purchase a band and outfit, and Idaho presents free ranges, with water from the mountain streams and timber to shelter from the burning sun in summer and the inclement weather in winter. Opportunities are sometimes presented where bands can be leased for a term of years on the share system, where the sheep are furnished by the owner to be cared for by the lessee, who returns to the lessor one-half the wool clippings and half the increase and the original number at the end of the term. Many poor men have become wealthy and independent who began sheep raising on the lease system. An illustration presents itself in that of a herder who, without a dollar, obtained a four years' lease on 1,000 head of sheep. In the first year the increase was nearly 2,000; the second, 2,250; the last, 2,400, when the band numbered, less all losses, 7,000, an increase of 6,000 for the term. The receipts from one-half the wool to the owners was $650, $1,000 and $1,100 in consecutive years; the last year's wool clip was worth $4,500. The owner of the sheep during the four years had realized 3,000 sheep worth $10,000 and $5,000 from the wool; all from one-half the profits on 1,000 sheep. Like successful results have been common in Idaho. It is unnecessary to enumerate the many instances where the stock raiser began with his own capital. There are well-known men in Idaho who began without a dollar and by their own tact and energy are now able to count their success by many thousands of dollars.

The number of sheep in Idaho is about 470,000. There has been a marked increase in the number of improved sheep and in the yield and quality of the wool. The average fleece is about six pounds in weight and is eagerly purchased by buyers for the Eastern markets. The Idaho mutton also finds favor in the markets East, and thousands are shipped over railways or driven overland to Omaha and other points.

FRUITS.

The fruits produced in the Northwest are noted for their extraordinary beauty, size and quality. Of all the many surprises which Idaho presents to Eastern visitors, nothing strikes them with greater astonishment than a first sight of the fruits in their season, in the orchards and grounds in the fruit belt of the state, extending from British Columbia on the north to Utah and Nevada on the south. The apples, pears, peaches, apricots, prunes, plums, cherries and all small fruits are grown in perfection. The quality of the fruit is excellent, the size large and the yield enormous. It is the size and yield which strikes the beholder with surprise. Apples may be seen from 12 to 16 inches in circumference; peaches, 10 to 12 inches; plums and prunes, 4 to 6 inches, and cherries and all other fruits in like proportion. The long fruit-bearing limbs, hidden with crowded fruit, hang perpendicularly on account of the enormous weight. This is especially true of plums and prunes, a single year's growth of limb bearing hundreds of the fruit.

Young trees grow very rapidly on being planted in the orchard and bear shortly afterward. The young bearing wood growing to great lengths, the quality of fruit one will sustain is almost incredible to those unacquainted with the fruit-bearing habits of trees west of the Rocky Mountains. It is owing to these qualities of Idaho fruit that wonderful productions are obtained from orchards. A four-years' growth of young trees

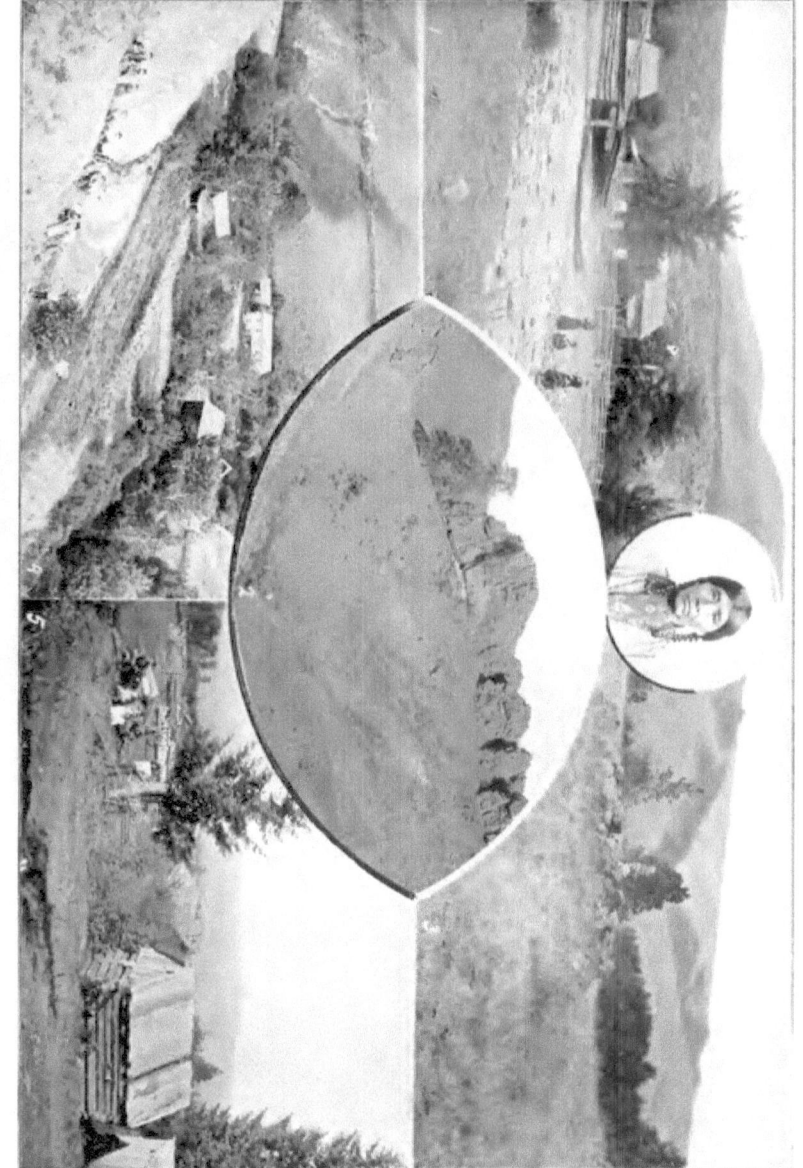

HISTORIC PICTURES IN IDAHO COUNTY

No. 1—State Creek Stockade, Where 200 Persons Took Refuge During the Indian War of 1877. No. 2—White Bird Battle Ground, Where 36 Soldiers, Under Colonel Perry, Were Killed, June 17, 1877. No. 3—Clearwater Battle Ground, Where 13 Soldiers and 15 Indians Were Killed, July 11, 1877. No. 4—John Day Ranch, Scene of Indian Massacre, June 14, 1877. No. 5—"Camp Howard" Overlooking Camas Prairie. No. 6—Too Lah the Friendly Nez Perce Squaw Who Warned the Settlers of the Outbreak of 1877.

FROM PHOTOS BY SIEGMAN, MOSCOW.

IRRIGATION SCENES IN IDAHO.

LARGE ROLLER MILLS AT WEISER — STREET IN WEISER

SCENERY IN BEAR LAKE COUNTY.

No. 1 — Natural Bridge, Bear Lake Hot Springs.   No. 2 — Fish Haven, from Summer Residence of Hon. Chas. B. Wilson.   No. 3 — Jar's Gap, Two and One-half Miles from Montpelier.   No. 4 — Bear Lake, Showing the Wonderful Natural Roadway Between Bear and Mud Lakes.

have yielded: apple trees, 200 pounds; cherries 75 pounds; peaches, 150 pounds; pears, 130 pounds; plums, 150 pounds. These are not exceptional figures, but are duplicated in many well-cultivated young orchards in the state. Small fruits, such as strawberries, currants, raspberries, blackberries, etc., are also very prolific. The more hardy fruits can be grown with success in most all of the higher elevations of the state. There are fruit farms which contain many thousands of trees with many acres devoted to the cultivation of small fruits, and the planting goes on each year, the demand keeping well up to the supply. It is seldom a crop failure occurs, and then only partially. There are orchards in the state that produce from 20,000 to 50,000 bushels of fruit annually.

The grape succeeds admirably and attains high perfection in size and quality; the soil being peculiarly adapted to the thorough development of its best qualities for the table use and wine making. For drying fruits, the climate is well adapted to this branch of fruit culture. Nowhere does the Italian prune attain such perfection as in Idaho; the dried prune being thought to be of better flavor and quality than the best importations from Italy. The universal demand for dried and canned fruits will always maintain the importance of fruit growing as a profitable business in Idaho.

UNITED STATES PUBLIC LANDS.

There are about 7,500,000 acres of government public land in Idaho open to settlement in the United States Land Office. These are located as follows: The western district at Boise City, the southern central district at Hailey, the eastern district at Blackfoot. These are traversed by the Union Pacific. The northern central district at Lewiston, on the Snake River, is reached by boat, and the northern district, at Cœur d'Alene, is traversed by the Union Pacific and the Northern Pacific Railway systems. The Indian reservations contain about 1,500,000 acres, which include some of the finest agricultural lands. These reservations are occupied by the Blackfoot, Lemhi, Nez Perce and Cœur d'Alene Indians. As fast as the Indian occupants can be induced to accept lands in severalty, the remaining lands will be opened to settlement.

STATE PUBLIC LANDS.

By the act admitting Idaho as a state, Congress donated to the state, in trust, for certain public purposes, in addition to Sections 16 and 36 previously reserved for school purposes, 700,000 acres, of which about 160,000 acres have been selected by the state and are subject to disposal. The remainder will be secured for the state as fast as the difficult work of selection can be done. Congress, with proper foresight, has fixed the minimum price of these lands at $10 per acre. The state has provided by law for the appraisement and sale of the lands to which title has been perfected. Much of the lands heretofore sold have realized prices greatly exceeding the limit fixed by the act of Congress. Sales of school lands have realized an average of $23.91. This will convey to the reader an idea of the vast sum the munificent grant will produce with proper management.

COMMERCE.

The commerce of Idaho is confined almost wholly to railway traffic and by navigable waters. The Union Pacific systems traverse the southern and northern parts of the state; the Northern Pacific and the Great Northern also traverse the latter part. The united length of this network of railway lines in the state is enormous. The Snake, Cœur d'Alene, Kootenai, Clarke's, Pend d'Oreille, Clearwater and other rivers each furnish some facilities for navigating the interior, as also do some of the larger lakes. These waters are of great importance to the districts in which they are located. There are also within the state 92,618 miles of telegraph lines to transmit communications to and from all parts of the world reached by wire. The exports consist of the products of mining and agriculture chiefly, and the imports include nearly every article demanded by the wants of the population.

MANUFACTURES.

Idaho with her mountains stored with inexhaustible sources of wealth, with her iron, copper, coal and other minerals, her forests of timber unexcelled, with vast quantities of peltry, wool, ores and other raw materials, has not as yet drawn enterprise and capital to enter upon their transformation into manufactured articles of use and necessity. But in time, probably not far distant, the now valuable treasures will be dragged from their undisturbed recesses, the hides will be prepared for their uses, the wool will be transformed into articles of apparel and the ores reduced for useful purposes. Everywhere among the streams is found sufficient power to run the looms of the world which is now utilized only by a few flouring mills to transform immense wheat crops, and a few saw mills in manufacturing lumber.

Idaho is open to many enterprises which might be found profitable. Materials for the manufacture of glass and pottery ware are plentiful. Good points can be found where foundries, machine shops, soap factories, tanneries, lumber mills, planing mills, sash and door factories; flouring mills of improved patterns can be located with an advantage to the consumer and the manufacturer.

MINING.

Mining is the leading industrial pursuit in Idaho. It is estimated that there are 40,000 persons whose occupation is devoted to this industry. The production of the mines in the state in the year 1892 was of gold, approximately $2,000,000; silver, $4,000,500. The lead product is very great, Idaho being in the front rank in the production of this metal. The extensive copper mines lie undeveloped and unproductive on account of the distance from transportation. A special chapter on minerals and mining will be found in this work, to which the reader is referred for extended and valuable information on this interesting industry.

ROADS.

The importance of good roads is nowhere better realized than by the people of Idaho. The state has inaugurated a system for the construction of state roads to penetrate the more important sections of the state needing highways, which could not otherwise be constructed without entailing onerous charges on the people. Some of these roads are under construction and others in contemplation awaiting surveys. The necessity and justice of the state assuming the task of constructing and maintaining these great thoroughfares which traverse mountainous regions are apparent, as the development of its wealth and future prosperity depend largely on easy communications to all parts of its territory.

CHURCHES.

The religious sentiment in the state is represented by all churches and denominations. Church buildings have been erected in all settlements where the inhabitants were sufficiently able to build them. The Episcopalian, Methodist and Methodist Episcopal Church South, Presbyterians, Baptists and Roman Catholics are the leading denominations in the number of ownerships of churches. Many others have edifices of worship. The church of Latter Day Saints has a large following in the southeastern part of the state.

PUBLIC BUILDINGS.

New in statehood, Idaho has as yet few public buildings. The attention of her people has already been directed to the erection of necessary buildings for state purposes. The Capitol is located in the beautiful city of Boise, an account of which will be given with Ada County. The Penitentiary is also located there. The Insane Asylum is located at Blackfoot in Bingham County. References to other institutions, educational and charitable, have been made elsewhere.

IDAHO=THE GEM OF THE MOUNTAINS.

GROWTH.

It was not until the discovery of the Oro Fino Creek mines that public attention was directed to the great mining wealth of Idaho. Immigration tended to seek homes near the coast, where communication with the world could be had by the ocean, rather than by the dangerous, lengthy trails overland. When the news reached the settlements the people flocked to the new El Dorado, and at once the development of mining and the growth of Idaho began, since which time it has been steadily onward. In the nineteen counties organized when the census of 1890 was taken, the report gives the population of each as follows:

The completion of the Union Pacific Railway in 1869 stimulated emigration from all quarters to the West, which was increased by the completion of the Oregon Short Line through Idaho and the Oregon Railway and Navigation Company's line in 1883:

COUNTIES.	POPULATION.
Ada	8,384
Alturas	2,626
Bear Lake	6,061
Bingham	13,492
Boise	3,471
Cassia	3,135
Custer	2,196
Elmore	1,870
Idaho	2,965
Kootenai	40,337
Latah	9,129
Lemhi	1,916
Logan	5,151
Nez Perce	2,598
Oneida	6,827
Owyhee	2,971
Shoshone	5,537
Washington	3,588
Indians and soldiers	3,551
Total	90,549

It is evident to all well-informed persons that the report is placed too low by about 10,000.

The assessment for taxation for the year 1892 shows an increase in value of all property over that of 1890 of $5,578,761.

The following table shows the taxable valuation of real and personal property for the year 1892:

COUNTIES.	VALUATION.
Ada	$5,032,713
Alturas	664,142
Bear Lake	1,011,125
Bingham	6,120,951
Boise	641,997
Cassia	760,000
Custer	650,850
Elmore	2,117,851
Idaho	1,296,453
Kootenai	2,351,350
Latah	4,388,114
Lemhi	1,048,578
Logan	1,936,767
Nez Perce	1,698,579
Oneida	1,493,449
Owyhee	946,431
Shoshone	1,551,303
Washington	1,648,113
Total	$31,160,066

The assessment rolls do not represent all the property in Idaho. Lands unpatented and those unsurveyed, though many acres are under a high state of cultivation and improvement, are not taxed, and will yield no revenue to the state until surveyed and patented. Mines, representing a value of over $50,000,000, are not taxed. Considering that property is not assessed greater than 50 per cent of its true value, the assessment roll does not exhibit more than one-fourth of the actual wealth of the state.

In 1892 the assessed value of taxable property was $31,131,945
In 1890 the assessed value of taxable property was 24,288,399

Increase in 5 years $9,893,553

The receipts from all resources for the year 1892 were . . . $421,591 73
Disbursements for the year 328,795 58

$98,721 15

The receipts for the year 1891 . . . . $521,215 25
Disbursements 427,901 55

Balance $73,114 10

Showing an increase of receipts of $93,204 60
The bonded indebtedness on Dec. 31, 1892, was $251,000.

EDUCATION.

The advantages to a state in having an educated and intelligent population is fully realized by the people of Idaho. Just having entered upon the responsibilities of statehood, the legislature has been liberal in providing means for educational purposes. The common school system, perhaps not yet fully perfected, so far has been as efficient as could be expected. The fine public school buildings which have been erected in the cities and the towns, and the comfortable houses in the rural districts, are the pride of the people, whose liberality and progressiveness heretofore are assurances that the facilities for education throughout the state will rank high in the early future. With the liberal donations by Congress, estimated to be about 3,500,000 acres, the common school fund derived from their sale will be very great. This fund will remain a trust in the care of the state for the use of present and future generations. To this will be added special funds derived from sources fixed by the legislature. The amount levied for school purposes in the state by taxation in the year 1890 was $102,800. In the year 1892 the amount raised was $320,235, an increase in one year of $118,655. The entire school population in 1890 was 25,741, and the report for 1892 shows a school population of 31,219, an increase in two years of 5,478.

Congress did not neglect the higher grades of scientific and practical education, for liberal grants were made to the state to encourage and aid the establishment of institutions for such purposes. The grant for the State University was 50,000 acres. The legislature has provided for its establishment, and it is located at Moscow, in Latah County. A building has recently been completed, sufficient, it is hoped, for present needs. It was opened for students in October, 1892, with an auspicious beginning. An agricultural college having a grant of 90,000 acres of land, a state normal school and a scientific school, each having land grants of 100,000 acres, will be established as soon as available funds can be realized. For the purpose of establishing an asylum for the care and instruction of the deaf, dumb and blind, there was granted 150,000 acres. Agricultural experimental stations are located at Idaho Falls, Nampa and Grangeville. These are for scientific pursuits in all matters pertaining to the realms of agriculture and horticulture.

IDAHO'S SCHOOL LANDS.

Their Value, and How They May be Obtained.

By Hon. F. A. Fenn, Chief of Land Department.

The future of Idaho as regards educational facilities and advantages is most promising. The munificent grant of land made to the state by the general government, coupled with the minimum price (f10 per acre) at which state lands may be sold, assures an endowment amply sufficient to defray all expenses of the public schools. The amount received from the sale of school lands goes into the general school fund, which is irreducible, the interest derived from its investment in state bonds and farm mortgages being alone available for the support of the schools. This interest, after but one year's operation of the law providing for sales of land, amounts to over $10,000 per annum. The first school land was sold Nov. 27, 1892, and the last, Oct. 10, 1892. The gross amount of sales made during that time was $617,470 17, an average of $13.92½ per acre. When it is remembered we have belonging to the state, under the grant for common schools, nearly 3,500,000 acres, an idea of the magnitude of our school fund in the near future can be formed. Within five years, it is confidently expected that the common schools of the state will be entirely supported by the income from the state fund, and local taxation, except for extraordinary purposes, will not be known in connection with our public schools. The gross amount paid teachers in the state for the school year ending Sep. 1, 1892, was $193,442 44. (See Section 15, Annual Report Superintendent Public Instruction for 1890-91.) More than one-fourth of the amount of teachers' salaries is now paid by the income of the school funds created by the sale of lands during one year. The salaries, too, here mentioned included those paid high school teachers. Were the salaries restricted to common schools, the percentage paid by the income of state funds would be still greater.

Other educational institutions are, like our common schools, munificently endowed. The University, located at Moscow, has a grant of 50,000 acres which at the minimum price of f10 per acre, means an irreducible fund for this institution of at least $500,000. Very much of the land will sell for twice or thrice the minimum, so that the University may safely be said to have $1,000,000 represented by her grant of lands.

IDAHO—THE GEM OF THE MOUNTAINS.

The last legislature established two normal schools, one at Lewiston in the north, and one at Albion in the south. The grant for the support of these schools is 100,000 acres, and assures for the teachers of Idaho opportunities for technical training in normal schools equal to the best in the Union.

The vast agricultural resources of the state demand the highest instruction for those who would achieve the best results in the farming industry. This is made certain by the 90,000 acres grant for the Agricultural College. This grant is being distributed over the entire state in the selections made under the direction of the State Board of Land Commissioners. The arid plains of Southern Idaho, which are transformed from a desert waste to an Eden by the magic water of the Snake River; the bunch grass hills of Latah, Nez Perce and Idaho counties, where bountiful Nature provides ample rainfall to insure unfailing cereal crops unrivaled by the yields of any other spot on earth; the practically inexhaustible forests of the northern and eastern portion of the state, are all being made to yield of their choicest for the benefit of the various institutions. No state in the Union has such variety of natural resources. Its agricultural productions range from some tropical fruits grown in the Lower Snake River Valley, to the grains and vegetables adapted to the higher temperate climates. The location in the high latitude is, by the uninformed, deemed detrimental to moderate climatic conditions. The altitude above the sea, ranging from 600 to 8,000 feet, gives variety, while the warm winds, locally called Chinook winds, moderate the temperature and render the climate equable. While during last winter (1892-3) unusual snows and extreme cold afflicted the most favored portions of the Mississippi Valley, Boise City, in the midst of the Snake River Valley, at no time during the winter had to exceed three inches of snow. This was the deepest, and lasted for two days. That Boise City is not an exceptional locality in this regard may be shown by the fact that, on the first day of November, 1892, the writer plucked from the bushes and ate ripe raspberries, and ate, in the garden where it grew part of a ripe, luscious watermelon. This occurred in the garden of Mr. Theodore Swarts of White Bird, in the northern part of Idaho County.

The casual observer, by examination of a map of Idaho, would determine that all of Central Idaho is a region so rough and mountainous as to be utterly uninhabitable and valueless. No greater error could possibly be made. During the summer season those mountains afford unsurpassed pasturage for vast herds of stock that in the winter subsist on the hay so abundantly produced in the valley. These mountains are clothed with vast forests of the choicest timber, fir, red cedar, white and yellow pine and tamarack, excelling the famous pineries in Michigan and Maine and equaling the fir regions of Puget Sound. Then, again, beneath the surface of these mountains are found mineral deposits, gold, silver, copper and lead, the richness of which makes Idaho the peer of Colorado and Montana as a mineral producer.

The selection of large tracts of land in all parts of the state, in satisfaction of the grants made by the United States, affords to colonies opportunities to secure thousands of acres of lands in a body for the establishment of homes, for the acquisition of lands under the most favorable conditions. While the minimum price, fixed by the constitution of the state, may appear high, it in reality is not. No residence upon the land is required; but one-tenth of the purchase price must be paid at the time of purchase, the remainder running for ten years at 6 per cent interest, the purchaser, however, having the option of paying any part or the whole of the purchase price at any time. The land is taxable only to the extent of the paid-up interest of the purchaser in the land. The policy of the state is to allow the land to remain as security for the irreducible fund for the creation of which the land was granted. The state can use only the income, and therefore the interest alone is required to be paid promptly. The one-tenth exacted at the time of purchase is but an evidence of good faith. The state certificates of sale are assignable, and to all intents and purposes, so long as interest is kept paid up, are as good as a deed to property practically exempt from taxation.

This leads me to say that an erroneous impression may easily be formed as to the rate of taxation and the actual value of property throughout the state. The rate may appear excessive, but when considered in connection with the very low assessments, it is not. The average assessed value of lands the state over, as shown by examination of the State Auditor's report for 1892, is less than $5 per acre, while the average price received for school lands sold at public auction in all parts of the state was for the year ending Oct. 10, 1892, $23.91 per acre. (See report State Board Land Company, page 30.) The lands sold were unimproved, either covered with sagebrush, requiring to be cleared, as in the southern part of the state, or in its native bunchgrass sod, necessitating the expenditure of from $2 to $3 per acre for breaking and cultivation, as in the northern part, while the lands assessed were all improved and to a great extent in the very highest state of cultivation. Still, with the great difference in condition, the actual selling price of unimproved lands was almost five times as great as the assessed value of the improved property. Causes, too numerous for discussion in this brief item, conduce to the anomalous condition which appears to exist, making Idaho seem the poorest of states burdened with excessive taxation. Were property assessed at its true value, the rate of taxation would be reduced so low as to be inconsiderable.

When the foregoing article is carefully considered, is it not true that Idaho will become one of the leading educational centres of the United States? To-day the "Gem State" surprises everyone with the rapid advancement made in her educational facilities during the last decade. Look back but a few years and compare the log hut with the beautiful structures in which our children now are taught. We believe we have a just right to be proud of our school record.

MINES AND MINING.

This topic has been pretty thoroughly treated in the separate sketches given of the several counties of the state, since there is not one of these counties that does not contain within its borders deposits of the precious metals and other valuable minerals. There remains but little that can be added in detail concerning this important resource and industry. As Idaho has fully proved herself one of the great natural treasure houses of the Nation, perhaps a scientific reader and practical mineralogist would first like to know something of her geological formation and of the kinds of rock that form the homes of her gold and silver bearing ledges. There has been as yet no regularly authorized scientific geological survey of the state, so that knowledge of her rock structure is restricted to what has come from the personal observation and experience of the prospector and miner in the thus far comparatively shallow and partial explorations made beneath the surface of the mountain rocks in their practical operation. These observations and partial examinations have sufficed to form a concensus of opinion among miners that the present condition of the surface is a result, in the first place of volcanic upheavals, followed by the grinding power of the primeval glaciers and finished by the washings by the mighty floods that accompanied the close of the glacial era. The entire area of the state is a vast elevated plateau, varying in altitude from 640 feet at Lewiston to 10,000 feet in the eastern part, and in the mountain sections almost every geological epoch is represented. What is familiarly known among miners as the country rock is granite, slate, porphyry and limestone in their various combinations; that of porphyry forming oftenest the casing of ledges. The lava formation is found chiefly underlying the deep alluvial of the valleys, revealing itself in the perpendicular walls of the deep river canyons and cropping out in cliffs and columnar formations along the sides and on the crests of the lower elevations and hills contiguous to the valleys. Thus, omitting technical geological terms and tedious scientific descriptions of formations, we have the general framework of the structure in which has been found the mineral treasures which have added and which continue to add so much to the wealth of the Nation. Much of the history of the earlier and later operations of mining in Idaho, as well as of the present status of this industry, will be found elsewhere in this work. For many years, the working of the numerous rich placer deposits engrossed almost exclusively the attention of the miner. Gold in this form was so easily found, and its extraction involved comparatively so little time and expense, that there was but little temptation to look further. But the placer deposits could not last always. As the process of exhaustion went on, it was leaving the miner with a past that had been golden, with a present that was daily becoming more unsatisfactory, and with a future that would have been a gloomy blank but for his knowledge of the fact that this placer gold upon which he had been reveling was but the offspring of the ledges from which the quartz that had contained it had been broken off during the ages, and that the gold freed by the crumbling of the ledges had, by the action of the waters, been diffused among the boulders, sand and gravel, where they had found it. Having devoured the offspring, which he had found so palatable and so easy of digestion, the voracious and still hungry miner next turned his attention to the parent ledges, which offered, it is true, greater resistance to his attacks, but which promised greater permanence to the supply and a longer lease to the field of his operations. It must not, however, be taken as literally true that placer mining has ceased to be prosecuted as a regular business or ceased to be a source of wealth in Idaho. There yet remain in most of the old mining districts considerable areas of good placer ground, where large numbers of men find profitable employment, and where the results continue to be quite satisfactory. Much of this area is virgin ground, which has to be reached and worked by the construction of new ditches and by the application of better methods and constantly improving facilities and machinery. A still greater area is ground that was worked by crude processes during the first years of placer mining in the creeks and gulches, when the sand and gravel from various deposits was rapidly and carelessly washed through short flumes and much of the gold lost in the "tailings" or *debris* that passed off in the process of washing. This is true in regard to many districts, but notably so in the Boise Basin, where only the lack of needed capital has prevented the inauguration of a system of bed-rock flumes, which ere this would have added millions to the annual output of the yellow metal. To these sources of placer gold must be added the bars and gravel deposits along the entire course of Snake River, where placer gold has been found at almost every point in paying quantities, but where the particles of gold are of such minute fineness that the persevering miner has been nearly baffled in his efforts to save them. In many instances, however, a very encouraging degree of success has attended these enterprises. The miners know that the gold is there, and they have determined that it must be saved, and the truth of the saying, that "Necessity is the mother of Invention," is being constantly exemplified and illustrated in discovering and applying better methods for saving this fine gold. Even under these adverse conditions, the Snake River placers have already added materially to the gross yield of gold in the state. As the area covered by these placers is of very great extent, and as the deposits are practically inexhaustible, they must prove an ever-increasing and permanent source of wealth. It would be a needless waste of time to mention in detail all the districts in which quartz mines have been opened and worked, or to attempt to sketch a history of mining operations and the results that have attended them. It will suffice to say that in almost every instance, where good management and persistent industry have characterized these operations, good and satisfactory results have been obtained, and in many cases the owner has reaped a rich reward for his enterprise and labor. The causes of failure in most cases, where there has been failure, can be directly traced to gross mismanagement and needless waste and extravagance. Of course, the high cost for labor, provisions, mining supplies of every kind, and for transportation during the earlier period of quartz mining, caused many mines that have since proved to be valuable properties to be abandoned. From the first discovery of the precious metal-bearing veins in the mountains of Owyhee down to the present time, no one at all conversant with the situation has ever doubted the permanence of these veins nor their great extent and richness. Now that the facts have been made patent to the whole mining world, and the great wealth of these mines demonstrated beyond a possibility of doubt in any quarter, astonishment is everywhere expressed that these mines were not continuously worked during the long period that has elapsed since they were first opened. Still, the causes we have enumerated, and the additional fact that it was found impracticable to attract the attention of capitalists to them, sufficed to put a quietus on quartz mining and to bring on a long period of somnolence, from which the country has but recently awakened. In Boise County, where numbers of rich ledges have long been known to exist, and indeed in every other quartz-mining district in the state, the same causes have produced precisely similar conditions. In Boise County, however, we have one of the notable instances in which good management and persistent enterprise and industry have fully demonstrated what these qualities can accomplish. The Gold Hill Mine at Quartzburg contains no richer ore bodies than have been found in several other mines on the same belt; yet the Gold Hill has been continuously and successfully operated for more than twenty years with results that have made the owners wealthy, while operations in the neighboring mines have been spasmodic, uncertain and generally unproductive of profitable results. Although the working of these and silver-bearing quartz veins is yet in its infancy in Idaho, enough has been done to prove that the mining industry will continue to be a permanent source of wealth, and that the output from mining operations will continue to increase from year to year for an indefinite time to come. As yet explorations and developments have only been partial. Vast mountain areas remain unprospected and almost unvisited and unknown. The broad mineral-bearing belt is known to be continuous entirely across the state, by the discoveries that have been made at the various points along its course, and wherever seen and examined the mountain region has been found to be seamed with metal-bearing veins. No other conclusion is rational than that many other rich mines remain yet undiscovered. The number of galena veins, containing in abundance what is known as lead-silver ores, are beyond computing. Many of this class of mines have been opened and worked with varying degrees of success in widely separated sections of the state, notably in the Wood River and Cœur d'Alene regions. The future of these mines and their value it is difficult to predict and estimate, further than that it is certain they will continue to be worked, as much capital is already invested in them, and they are known to be rich in both the quantity and quality of the ores they contain. The market value of the bullion to be produced from them is another thing, as this, unfortunately, is made to depend upon the kind of future legislation that will influence the value of both silver and lead. It is reasonable, however, to hope that right counsels will prevail in the end, and that both metals will be restored to their rightful place and value; in which event, the silver and lead products from this class of mines in Idaho will alone make the young state one of the richest in the Union. Besides the mines of gold and silver and the lead found in combination with silver ores, Idaho includes among her productions all the other metals and mineral substances known to general commerce. Extensive and rich deposits of copper ore are found near Snake River in Washington County, and also in other sections of the state. Only the fact that these deposits are found in isolated localities, remote from present lines of railway communication, has prevented them from being developed and made productive. Coal of excellent quality has also been found in various sections, where, as explorations show far show, the fields are extensive. Iron ore in large deposits, and with a large percentage of that indispensable metal, is found in proximity to the coal fields and ready to be worked into all its needed forms whenever enterprise aided by capital shall begin the work of appropriating and utilizing these gifts of Nature. As regards the total Idaho gross value of the yield from all the mines in Idaho since the beginning of mining operations within the boundaries of the state, there has never been any reliable *data* from which even an approximate estimate could be made. A very large percentage of this gross yield was the result of placer mining. Comparatively little of this gold went through any channel or into any place where its value could be accurately known, as the miners and traders made no report of the results of their labors or of their business transactions; so that the sources of official and statistical information were meager, and were confined for the most part to what could be gleaned from the books of express companies and the reports of transactions in the mints and assay offices. The same remark applies to much of the gold resulting from quartz mining, especially in the numerous instances where quartz mines were worked on a small scale. Official reports made a few years ago place the total yield at $200,000,000. This estimate, however, based on *data* gathered from strictly official sources, is much too small; but it will be seen by comparing the figures of all reports up to date that for several years past the annual output has been steadily increasing. When it is considered that Idaho has been the most isolated, the least known and the most neglected of any of the young communities of the West, and that she is surrounded by heavy bullion-producing states and territories where capital finds ready and profitable investment, it is by no means surprising that comparatively so little has been done and that so little is generally known of her magnificent mining resources.

PROSPECTING IN THE MINES.

"THE LOWER VALLEY" FROM SODA SPRINGS

PRINCIPAL BUILDINGS OF PARIS, COUNTY SEAT OF BEAR LAKE COUNTY.

No. 1—Paris Roller Mills.   No. 2—Mormon Tabernacle.   No. 3—Bear Lake County Courthouse.

Reproduced by Mr. Edward Smith.

IDAHO SCENERY.

No. 1—Ouig's Hind Legs, North Fork of Clearwater River. No. 2—Elk Creek, North Fork of Clearwater River. No. 3 —Wallowa Mountains and Snake River, from Slope of Seven Devils. No. 4—Looking Toward Lewiston, from Slope of Seven Devils. No. 5—Salmon River Mountains and Horse-shoe Bend. Snake and Salmon River Divide.

BLACKFOOT CATTLE COMPANY'S RANCH, NEAR SODA SPRINGS, A TYPICAL IDAHO SCENE.

IDAHO=THE GEM OF THE MOUNTAINS.

ADA COUNTY.

This county was created and organized at the second session of the Idaho Territorial Legislature, in the month of December, 1864, while the state capital of the young territory was yet at Lewiston, in Nez Perce County, where it had been temporarily located by the act of Congress organizing the Territory of Idaho. At the time of the creation of the then new county, the great area included within its boundaries was a portion of the large county of Boise, which at that time included the entire region now covered by the counties of Boise, Washington, Canyon and Ada. The successive divisions of this original large area and the creation of new counties at regular intervals during a short series of years show in a striking light the rapid increase in population and the no less rapid development of the natural resources of the country of which it formed a part.

Ada County was named in honor of a little daughter of Hon. H. C. Riggs. Mr. Riggs is one of Idaho's oldest pioneers, being at that time a resident of Boise County and representing his county in the legislature. By an act of the same session of the legislature, the capital of the territory was removed from Lewiston to Boise City, and thus the county of Ada became the capital county of the territory and subsequently of the state; a condition and relationship which has continued to exist to the present time. As at present diminished, and shorn of her former proportions, the county can only claim an area of some 1,500 square miles, with a population of something less than 8,000, but she is more than compensated for this by the absence of local rivalries, conflicting interests and antagonisms or differences of any kind among her people. She enjoys a most advantageous position, occupying the upper portion of the beautiful and fertile Boise Valley, with the rich *mesa* lands on the south, the greater part of the area of the county being good arable land of the best quality, provided with irrigating ditches, and much of it already covered with productive farms. Only a small percentage of the area is mountainous, and this mountain portion, lying on the north and east, is known to be rich in gold and silver bearing ledges, which only await the development which time must soon bring to make them an additional and important source of wealth to the county and to the state. It is generally conceded that Boise Valley, taken as a whole, enjoys a decided advantage over her sister valleys of Southern Idaho in point of climate and natural resources, and it is well known that the upper portion of this valley, as regards climate, is peculiarly favored. The snowfall is light all over the valley, while the cold is never intense, mercury seldom falling below zero; but the upper portion of the valley, by its sheltered position, is peculiarly exempt from even the slight rigors of an Idaho Valley winter, while the heat in summer, always tempered by cool mountain breezes, is seldom so great, either in degree or duration, as to make it a subject of complaint.

The exact financial condition of Ada County is somewhat difficult to arrive at, for the reason that the result of the legislation which divided the county the last time has left certain matters and questions incident to the division as yet unadjusted and unsettled. It is certain, however, that the final adjustment of these matters must leave Ada County in a healthy financial condition, as the county debt in any event will be small, while the resources of the county in the shape of taxable property are by far the largest and best of any in the state. The area devoted to agriculture and fruit growing has been longer under cultivation than that of any other section of the state, its irrigated ditches are the oldest in right to the water of the Boise River and have first access, while long and careful cultivation has brought all the older farms and a large percentage of the entire area to a good state of productiveness. Of the irrigated area within the Boise Valley proper, that is, the lands lying contiguous to the river and bounded by the bluffs and uplands on either side, there are, approximately, 25,000 acres. These lands are covered by the older canals and ditches which have been many years in use. Upon these lands are the oldest farms, in a good state of cultivation, producing fine crops of grain, hay and vegetables. South of the Boise River the country rises in broad benches or plateaus, sometimes called *mesas*, which up to a comparatively recent date were entirely arid and apparently sterile, causing it to be classified as a portion of the "Great Snake River Desert." The advent of irrigation, however, has changed much of this old-time arid and sterile desert into productive farms, meadows, orchards and gardens. The area thus reclaimed and cultivated will aggregate some 15,000 acres, giving a total of irrigated and cultivated lands within the county of about 40,000 acres.

The unirrigated lands consist, first of a belt of *mesa* lands on the south side of the river, located above the present completed canals, but below the line of what has been heretofore known as the "New York Canal." This enterprise may be now said to be in a condition of "suspended animation" for want of funds, but it is only a question of time when operations must be resumed, as too much money has already been expended upon it to allow the right to lapse or the enterprise to be abandoned. This belt of *mesa* lands will average about 3 miles in width, with an approximate length of 30 miles, extending from the Boise to the Snake rivers, giving at the lowest estimate 90,000 acres of land equal in fertility to the best sagebrush lands in the county and available for future homes as soon as water can be obtained.

North of the Boise River, and immediately contiguous to the cultivated area of the valley, there is a body of very rich uplands lying at present above the area that can be reached by the water now available in that quarter. This body of land will aggregate some 50,000 acres, and it will be reached and supplied with water by an extension of what is known as the "Walling Canal," an enterprise which during the past twenty-five years has supplied Boise City and vicinity with water, and has been the agent which converted the present site of the city from what was once an arid sagebrush plain to its present densely shaded and garden-like beauty. This canal, having served its original purposes, and having created a lovely and fertile oasis in an erstwhile desert, will now be enlarged and extended to the rich body of uplands below the city, where its life-giving potency is needed. This gives of irrigated lands 40,000 acres and of unirrigated lands 135,000 acres.

As regards the crops grown on these irrigated lands, it is somewhat difficult to give accurate statistics, as there has never been any systematized effort made in the way of collecting *data*. In general it may be stated that the crops upon which reliance is mainly placed are those of hay, fruit and vegetables. These crops are cultivated in preference to those of the cereals, on account of the smaller outlay and greater profit attending production. The soil is well adapted to the growth of wheat, oats and barley, while even Indian corn succeeds very fairly. Thirty bushels of wheat per acre and 40 bushels per acre of oats and barley is not an unusual result, though perhaps a little over the average. Of hay, the red clover will yield two crops per season and give two tons per acre for each cutting. Alfalfa does still better, giving three cuttings with a like result per acre. Taking one season with another, the market price of this hay will average at least $7.50 per ton, the price having often been during recent years as high as $10 per ton.

Opinion is divided somewhat with regard to the most profitable fruit to grow. To cultivate a variety seems to be thought the best rule to follow. Prunes, however, are undoubtedly the favorite crops, and the returns from this fruit, realized and verified here in numerous instances, seem almost incredible. From a recent report of the City Auditor, written and submitted here where all the facts are familiar, we quote the following: "A conservative estimate is that a five-year-old prune tree will bear 400 pounds worth two cents per pound on the tree. An acre of ground will plant 160 trees. The value of a prune crop from one acre is then seen to be $1,280. There are three varieties of prunes in this section, Italian, French and Silver, but the former does the best and is generally planted." Though the "prune fever" has but recently taken hold of the people here in earnest, we are nevertheless able to count within a radius of three miles from the centre of the city nearly 300 acres now cultivated in prunes, on most of which area the trees are already in bearing. It will be readily seen that with a soil and climate so admirably adapted to the cultivation and careful preparation of this fruit for already existing markets, this industry alone will constitute a constantly increasing source of wealth to the people of this highly favored section. The demand for this fruit is practically unlimited, and with better methods, larger facilities and lower rates of transportation, which must come in the early future, both the amount produced and the profits of the crop must increase very largely from year to year.

Whatever degree of truth and accuracy attaches to the saying that "Paris is France," may be applied with much more force and propriety to the newer saying that "Boise City is Ada County." The population of the county probably does not exceed 7,500 souls, of which the city of Boise claims 5,500, leaving 2,000 for all that portion of the county outside of the city.

Boise City.

Besides being the financial, commercial and political centre of Idaho, Boise City is widely known as one of the prettiest and healthiest cities in the country. The streets are wide and well kept, with well-constructed walks and crossings. Handsome trees line the streets, making the city delightfully cool and pleasant. A city ordinance for the erection of wooden structures within the fire limits has served to give the business portion a gratifying appearance of solidity. Many of the buildings of the city are really elegant specimens of metropolitan architecture in wood and stone. Boise City is the wealthiest city per capita in the United States, and ample evidence of the fact is to be seen in the residence portion, where handsome and costly buildings are by no means the exception. Broad lawns with well-kept grass and shrubbery attest the invigorating influence of water upon the river soil. Though the approach to the city by rail from Nampa is through a fertile country, where a very fair beginning has been made in the cultivation of the soil and the growth of fruit and shade trees it is always a matter of surprise when the first view of the city is obtained. So dense is the tree growth and foliage in and about the town that the entire mass of buildings, with the exception of a few tall spires, is hidden from view. To its beauty of position and to all its other many natural advantages and attractions, Boise City adds that of being the permanent seat of the state, county and municipal government. These taken together would insure permanent and continued prosperity and rapid growth even in a locality far less favored by Nature. Among the several institutions, either forming a portion of or connected and identified with the city, the first in order of the time of its establishment is the military post known as Boise Barracks. The establishment of this post antedates by a few weeks only that of the laying out and commencement of the city. United States troops have been permanently and continuously kept here since the establishment of the post, the reason being that besides being a central point for the movement of troops in case of need, troops can be kept here at a smaller cost to the government than at any other point, with the addition of being the healthiest post in the country.

The United States Assay Office is a large, commodious and conveniently constructed building, very substantially built of stone, at a cost to the government of $85,000.

For school and educational advantages, Boise deserves the title, that has often been bestowed by visitors, as being the Athens of Idaho. The city owns over $125,000 worth of school property, the property including an entire block in the very heart of the city, upon which has been erected one of the largest and finest school buildings in the Northwest, at a cost of $100,000. The cost of maintaining the school will approximate $25,000 annually. There are 15 teachers employed in the school, the principal receiving an annual salary of $1,500 and the teachers from $70 to $80 per month.

IDAHO=THE GEM OF THE MOUNTAINS.

* Besides the public schools there are two other very important educational institutions in the city: St. Teresa's Academy, under the direction of the Catholic Sisters of the Holy Cross, and St. Margaret's School, conducted under the auspices of the Episcopal Church. Both these institutions are devoted mainly to the education of young ladies, though both will receive and take good care of younger pupils of both sexes. Both institutions are supplying a need which could not otherwise be met, and both are doing noble work in the great cause of education.

Among other public buildings may be mentioned the State House or Capitol, erected while Idaho was yet a territory, at a cost to the people of the territory of $80,000. The building is perfect of its size and kind, complete in all its appointments and quite adequate for present demands.

Boise has three banks, the principal ones being the First National of Idaho and the Boise City National; the joint total assets of the two being $1,176,741.50. There is also the Capital State Bank of Idaho. This bank does a general banking business, the estimated wealth of its stockholders being $5,000,000. The total business done per month by these three banks is about $1,500,000.

What is known as the Rapid Transit Company, organized under a liberal charter from the city government, has inaugurated a system of electric street railway and already has three miles of track in successful operation. The aggregate cost of the work thus far is $87,000.

In the matter of railroads Boise is at present served by a branch of the Union Pacific from Nampa, a distance of 20 miles. This is far from being adequate or satisfactory, but it is a condition which cannot much longer continue. The city, by its commanding position, its political importance and its many natural features, has long been an object of attraction to other railroads. Everybody predicts a new era of railroad building in the early future, and with its advent Boise will be certainly reached by more than one competing line.

In addition to the irrigation canals, which have made Boise the scene of loveliness which it is, and which keep it green and blooming during eight months of the year, the city enjoys the unique privilege and advantage of being abundantly supplied with both cold and hot water obtained from artesian basins. The pure cold water from the artesian springs serves all domestic purposes for every house in the city, with enough to spare for jets and fountains, while the hot water from a depth of 400 feet and with a temperature of 180 degrees Fahrenheit, flows in sufficient volume to supply all the purposes of bathing and of heating buildings for a city of 30,000 inhabitants.

ALTURAS COUNTY.

The area embraced within the present limits of this county forms but a fragment of the great region once known as the original Alturas County. From this great area several counties have been successively carved, those of Custer, Elmore and Logan being the more recent slicings from her former grand domain. As she stands to day, Alturas County embraces within her boundaries but little more than the comparatively small section of mountainous country drained by the Wood River and its tributaries. Within these narrow limits, however, Nature has lavished her choicest gifts—of a mineral belt broad and rich, of numerous expanses of fertile land of heavily timbered forests, of large, beautiful lakes whose crystal waters reveal at wonderful depths moving masses of the finny tribes that furnish both sport and food for the delighted tourist and sojourner who come every summer to enjoy the bracing mountain air and the scenic beauties of mountain, stream and lake and sky, whose living pictures are nowhere on the green earth excelled. Although Alturas has been the victim of hostile and unjust legislation, which took from her so much of her rightful domain and left her with the burden of a debt which she has been obliged to pay with greatly diminished resources, and although she has also been the victim of many misfortunes and circumstances which have greatly retarded development, yet the brave little county has made a gallant fight, full of hope and faith in the bright future. "Few people," said Governor Shoup, in his report of 1890, "have ever met reverses with greater courage or struggled with larger zeal to overcome obstacles."

The mines of Alturas County belong to the lead-silver class, many of which have yielded quite largely and have brought fortunes to the lucky owners. A good feature of the mining industry in Alturas is the great number of mines which are worked profitably by their owners of moderate means. The average value of the lead-silver ores, according to the records kept by the leading assayer, is $160 per ton. The mining districts are fairly well supplied with quartz mills, smelters and other improvements and facilities, so that the large class of small producers have no great difficulty in realizing the results of their labors.

The county has several growing towns, Hailey and Ketchum being among the number. Hailey is the county seat and is the centre of a healthy trade. The town is well built and prosperous, notwithstanding the fact that it was almost entirely destroyed by fire a few years ago. Near Hailey are the famous warm springs, a favorite health resort, where $15,000 has been expended in the building of a fine hotel and improving and beautifying the grounds. Ketchum, situated 15 miles above Hailey, is the centre of trade for several groups of rich mines and the radiating point for trade and travel to the outlying camps north and east.

The agricultural development is all that could be expected in a region of such high altitudes, where the season of cultivation is necessarily short, but the soil is of such extreme fertility that the results are always satisfactory, and often surprising to those who witness the harvests for the first time. Compared with some of the great stock-growing counties of the state, the business of stock raising is limited in extent and in results. It is safe to state, however, that today there are but little less than 50,000 head of range stock in the county, with a corresponding number of horses, sheep and other domestic animals. With all these resources, which have been necessarily very briefly mentioned, and with all her many natural resources and advantages, the changed conditions which time must soon bring in the shape of cheap transportation, better prices for the products of her mines and an increase in her working population, a prosperous future for Alturas County cannot be doubted.

Hailey.

The town which has been and must continue to be one of the leading commercial centres of Idaho is Hailey, the county seat and political centre of Alturas County. This favored little city is situated in the beautiful Wood River Valley, which lies on the western slope of the Rocky Mountains. The resources of Hailey are not only her attractions from an agricultural, mining and lumbering standpoint, but the little metropolis has gained much notoriety through her magnificent capacities as a summer and health resort. In figuring the possibilities of building a city, the resources which are to make it must be carefully considered. This is what the good people would have the reader do, and then determine in his own mind as to whether this place could ever become a town of several times its present size. The following is what the citizens have to present as the resources of their place of residence. The mines constitute our backbone, and contain sufficient wealth to create a half-dozen old world empires. They yield gold, silver, copper, lead, iron, etc., at the rate of about $5,000,000 per annum, or over one-half the total output of the state.

The Hailey United States land district contains 19,000,000 acres, of which only about 750,000 have been surveyed. Of the surveyed land, nearly all of which is in Alturas and Cassia counties, not more than one-third has been taken up by settlers, and some of the finest farming land in the state—particularly on Camas Prairie, a few miles from Hailey—is yet open to settlement. Upon land similar to that last mentioned 60 bushels of wheat to the acre have been raised without irrigation, and other cereals, fruits and vegetables in the same proportion. The greater part of the land in this district requires irrigation; but rivers and creeks are plentiful, and the soil, when sufficiently watered, produces crops threefold larger than any of the Eastern states.

The growth of Hailey has been steady and sure, never of the mushroom character of so many Western towns, and with the magnificent agricultural resources developing hand in hand with her mining interest, this growth is continuous and will be permanent. The Methodist, Episcopal, Presbyterian and Roman Catholic churches are established, with earnest workers in the field of churchly endeavor. Our schools are our pride. Situated on a slight eminence overlooking the valley and river, we have built one of the "bulwarks of the republic," that reflects credit upon the community. The sightliest building in Hailey, it is also the handsomest and best appointed school building in Idaho. Its cost was only $35,000, but it is a much better building than could be secured almost anywhere else for twice the money. Pardon the further boast that we have the best corps of teachers in Idaho, for the best of reasons: We pay them more liberally than any other school district on the Pacific Slope.

Very few Western cities can, in candor, say much commendatory of their hotels. But it is the boast of all Wood Riverites, and confirmed by experienced travelers, that the Alturas and Merchants are thoroughly equipped, ably conducted hostelries. They are new, three-story, fireproof buildings, supplied with every modern improvement, such as electric lights, calls and annunciators, fire and burglar alarms, commodious and handsomely appointed lavatories, and the most elegant furnishings that money could buy. The Alturas represents an investment of $65,000, the Merchants about as much more.

Hailey being the seat of the vast and growing Alturas County, a commodious public building was a necessity, and in 1884 there was completed on a commanding site a three-story fireproof brick and stone structure costing $50,000, that serves as the repository of all the records of the county, a place for the sessions of the Second Judicial District Court, the Probate Court and for the safe incarceration of criminals.

Hailey has a complete system of water works, which furnishes an ample supply of pure mountain water, under a pressure of 120 feet, for all domestic purposes, and affords protection from fire. This enterprise has been a great factor in making Hailey the beautiful city that it is; its plentiful supply of water having rendered possible the green lawns and thrifty, luxuriant shade and fruit trees seen on every hand.

A company composed of a large number of ore producers owns the sampling works in Hailey. They have a daily capacity of 200 tons, which can be increased to 1,000 tons at a slight expense.

A branch of the Colorado Iron Works of Denver, located here, is fully equipped with foundry and machine shop to turn out promptly anything in its line, from a nail to a steam engine or a quartz mill. Its workmanship is unexcelled.

Apparently inexhaustible timber belts close at hand will supply all the mining and building lumber and cordwood that will be needed for generations. The forests that lie tributary to Hailey are alive with big and small game.

Hailey is lighted with electricity and the Brush-Swan is the system in use; and it is a notorious fact that Hailey streets and business houses are the best lighted of any city in the state.

The Rocky Mountain Bell Telephone Company has its central exchange for this region located here, whence wires radiate to all the mines, smelters and mills within a radius of 12 miles. Over 70 sets of instruments are in use.

One mile from Hailey are located the Hailey Hot Springs, now becoming famous as a resort for invalids, and especially those afflicted with mineral poisons or rheumatic troubles. Here are located the County Hospital and the Miners' Hospital, the latter supported by voluntary subscriptions of the miners.

IDAHO—THE GEM OF THE MOUNTAINS.

Ketchum.

BOISE COUNTY.

BINGHAM COUNTY.

River contain enough gold to pay the national debt, and of this kind of wealth Bingham County has a large proportion. The genius of man will certainly discover some means to rescue this great quantity of precious metal from its sandy bed." Bingham County has the honor of being the home county of Hon. Fred Dubois, one of the United States senators, who came to Idaho when quite a young man and went patiently to work at whatever honest occupation he could find, like the average young workers who have helped to build up this grand young commonwealth. In his case, as in that of others, industry and good conduct were soon rewarded in more ways than one. Mr. Dubois was not long in winning a high standard among his fellow citizens, and was appointed United States Marshal from Idaho Territory, was twice elected to Congress from the territory, and when Idaho put on the robes of statehood, among her first acts was that of placing upon the shoulders of the young statesman the senatorial toga. The county, though now shorn of her former grandeur, is still rich in resources of every kind, and has room and advantages for all who may come within her borders in search of homes and wealth.

BEAR LAKE COUNTY.

This, the smallest county in Idaho, occupies the southeast corner of the state, at an altitude of about 6,000 feet. The county is principally controlled by the Bear Lake Valley, which lies on the north and the south between mountain ranges, to the length of about 50 miles, varying in width from 10 to 15 miles. At the south end of the valley lies the beautiful Bear Lake, with an area of 12x18 miles. There are several small lakes within the county and many streams traverse the valley, which is magnificently adapted to grain growing, while the potato yields marvelously. Hardy fruits do well in all parts of the valley and grapes are particularly productive on the west shore of the lake. Cattle and sheep thrive in the foothills in the summer and the numerous natural meadows of the valley furnish plenty of hay for easy wintering. The first settlers here were colonists of the Mormon Church, who brought with them to the task of making homes in what was then a rugged and unpromising wilderness all the habits of the colony, industry and a perfect harmony of counsel in action which have always been distinguishing characteristics of the members of this church organization. The result is seen in the universal thrift of the people, in a population denser than in any other county of the state and a larger proportion of the soil under cultivation. Along the mountainous surface is a heavy growth of pine timber, into which the numerous saw mills of the county annually make inroads without seriously diminishing the supply.

The county supports several prosperous towns, among which may be named Montpelier, Paris, St. Charles and Fish Haven. The first named is the largest and is the principal trading point of the county, being on the line of the Union Pacific Railway. Paris is the county seat, and is situated on a stage line connecting with the Union Pacific at Montpelier. This is also a trading point of considerable importance. St. Charles, on the banks of Bear Lake, is a small village with many beautiful residences with home-like surroundings. Fish Haven lies on the west side of Bear Lake on the slope of the foothills, nestled among the trees and overlooking the water. From Fish Haven to the south there is a drive six miles long, through a shady lane which curves with the shore of the lake. This is one of the most home-like places in the State of Idaho, and is an ideal spot for a summer residence. The lake abounds in fish and is swarmed with dozens of species of birds varying in size from the snipe to the swan. The Bear Lake Hot Springs are on the northeast side of the lake and are destined to be known to the entire world. Here a stream of mineral water comes pouring from the side of the mountain, which is nearly boiling hot. A good hotel is maintained at this point, as are two splendid plunge-baths.

The Bear Lake Hot Springs.

RICH & AUSTIN, PROPRIETORS.

These celebrated springs are situated in Bear Lake County, State of Idaho, on the shore of Bear Lake, one of the most fascinating sheets of water in the Rocky Mountain region. The curative qualities of the waters of these springs are marvelous. For rheumatic complaints, skin diseases, catarrh and kindred ailments, they are unexcelled. The waters have never been fully analyzed, but sulphur, mercury and other exist in quantities sufficient to make the waters the best natural medical bath known. Montpelier, on the Oregon Short Line branch of the Union Pacific, is the most convenient railroad point. Hunting, fishing and boating are all combined with the resort, and a good family hotel, conducted by the genial J. C. Rich, a fairy-miner, affords abundance for the amusement. The place is about 6,000 feet above sea level, and affords one of the grandest scenic views of mountain, lake and valley to be found in the West. The springs are midway on the delightful carriage drive across the noted natural turnpike from Montpelier to Fish Haven, a beautiful villa on the western shore of Bear Lake, where the big-hearted Wilson takes care of his friends. Capitalists are invited to investigate.

Paris.

Paris, the county seat of Bear Lake County, lies on the west side of Bear Lake Valley, almost at the foot of Paris Peak. The town was the first settlement made in the valley and its date of inhabitance runs back to the year 1862. Ever since its earliest days it has been the principal Mormon town of Southern Idaho, and it is here that the beautiful tabernacle is situated which is illustrated on another page. This is the finest building in the State of Idaho.

The population of Paris is about 1,500. This town is surrounded upon three sides by fine farming lands, and the fourth side is the mountain, grazing and lumbering district.

MONTPELIER.

A Few Paragraphs Relative to the Metropolis of Bear Lake County.

A Thriving Manufacturing and Merchandising Town.

Just ten miles northeast of Paris, and near Bear River, lies the enterprising town of Montpelier. It is the principal business point and commercial centre of the fertile and prolific Bear Lake Valley.

The town is situated upon a gentle and almost imperceptible slope from the foothills, which break abruptly into the range of mountains that bound the valley on the east, like an impassable wall. To all other points of the compass lies a level, unbroken stretch of farming land, abundantly watered by the Bear River and its many small tributaries, from the never-exhausting mountain snows.

From the great canyon, at the very mouth of which Montpelier is nestled, a stream of considerable size flows, sparkling on its way, to empty its waters in the river beyond. This furnishes ample power for the flouring mills, moisture for the growing crops, orchards, groves and lawns, and drink for the inhabitants which compose the trade centre of this district.

Montpelier is the only railroad town of any importance in the valley, and is therefore necessarily the trade centre of this productive region. The population of about 1,500 people support the two commodious and elegant school buildings, which are to be found illustrated upon the page devoted to Montpelier.

A spacious opera house and a circulating library are numbered among the principal features of the town's principal attractions.

The Episcopalians, Presbyterians and Latter Day Saints each are represented among the religious denominations.

If the reader please, in connection with the foregoing, consider that this is a division terminal of the Union Pacific system where is located roundhouse and repair shops, many business houses, including a banking institution, together with an immense flouring mill. This is sufficient to acquaint the intelligent reader with the prosperity the town has enjoyed in the past.

It is from this point that daily stages traverse the sections that lie in the immediate vicinity. Stages leave here daily for Paris, Bloomington, St. Charles, Afton and Wyoming.

Montpelier's population is composed of an extraordinary intelligent and refined class of citizens, who, by their untiring efforts, have administered that town into an educational centre and leading business point. The immense amount of employment given by the Union Pacific Railway to industrious men, who make their homes here, gives Montpelier, in one point of view, the appearance of a manufacturing town. Not only is the employment of these men by the company a great financial benefit to the leading commercial town of Bear Lake County, but the beautiful homes that are added to Montpelier by its railroad men lend much to the architectural beauty of the place. We call special attention to the engravings in the Idaho Souvenir devoted to the town of Montpelier, which will portray a true idea of some of its representative public buildings.

As to the country tributary to Montpelier, we will refer the reader to an article devoted to Bear Lake County. It will be seen that the county is immensely rich and blessed with diversified resources. That which is of great interest to the traveler or tourist, and which may be found within the immediate vicinity of Montpelier, is the most superb scenery to be found upon the globe, which, together with the sparkling streams and peaceful lakes, lying at the foot of the towering precipices, presents to the observer a magnificent panorama of beauty and grandeur.

The municipal affairs of this favored little city are conducted in a neat commendatory manner. The best citizens are at the head of the government and every attention is given to the fulfillment of their duties. The City Council is alive to every proposition that comes from any source that will prove beneficial to the town.

The Post, a weekly paper, published by Mr. J. H. Wallis, is a bright and newsy publication, with a deserving circulation that reaches beyond what may be termed its own field. A sample copy of this excellent paper will give the reader a detailed report of matters of interest to himself, Montpelier and vicinity.

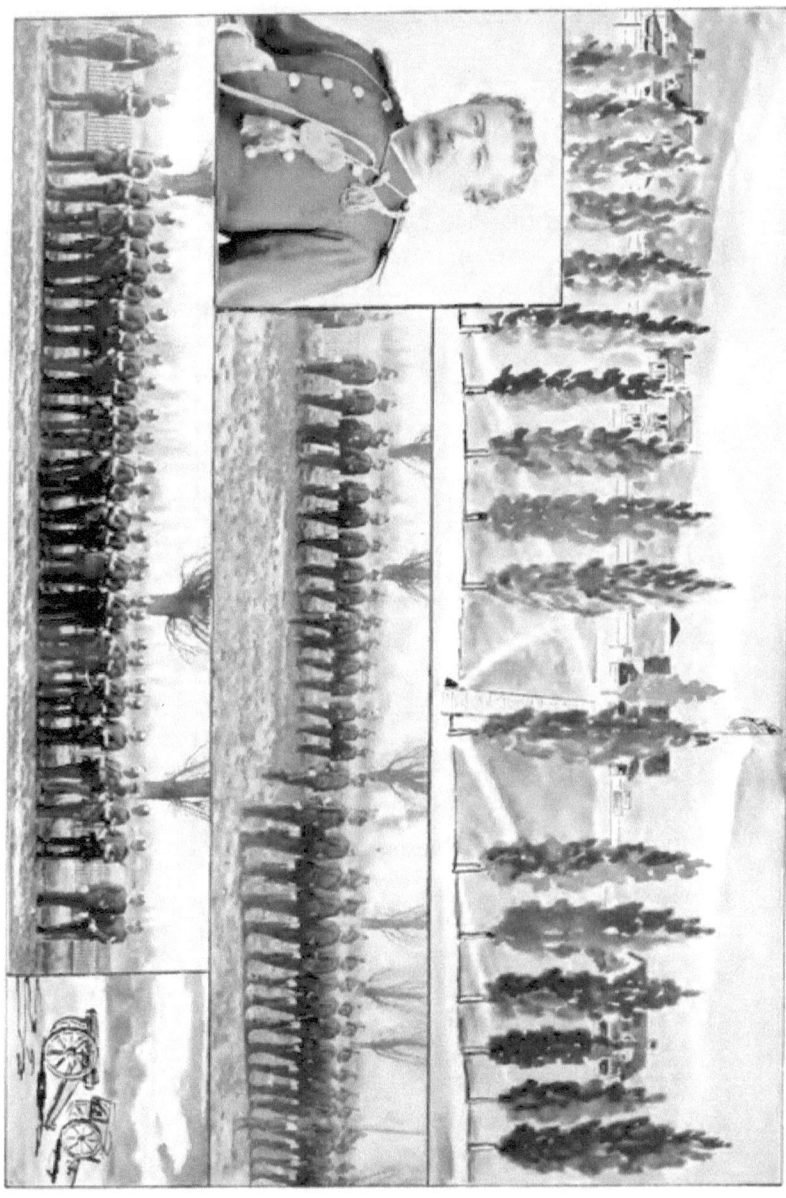

BOISE BARRACKS

Officers' Row—Major Kennedy, Commanding.—Troop of Cavalry, Captain Muncy.—Company of Infantry, Lieutenant Curtner.

PRINCIPAL BUILDINGS OF MONTPELIER, BEAR LAKE COUNTY.

No. 1—East Side School.   No. 2—West Side School.   No. 3—The Hotel Hunter.   No. 4—Residence of Mayor Edward Burgoyne.   No. 5—Building
of the Bear Lake Mercantile Company.   No. 6—Building of Mayor Ed Burgoyne's Mercantile Establishment.   No. 7—Montpelier Flouring Mill.

MONTPELIER POST BUILDING.

IDAHO'S FIRST BUILDING.

POST FALLS, ON THE SPOKANE RIVER.

BEAR LAKE HOT SPRINGS.

OVERLOOKING THE CITY OF CALDWELL — THE BOISE VALLEY FROM CANYON HILL.

IDAHO=THE GEM OF THE MOUNTAINS.

BANNOCK AND FREMONT COUNTIES.

The two new counties of Bannock and Fremont formed until recently portions of the county of Bingham, which was by the act of the second session of the state legislature divided so as to make three counties out of the original area. Since the creation and organization of the two new counties nothing has been done in the way of collecting statistical information with regards to them.

Bannock lies south of the present county of Bingham and covers an approximate area of 5,000 square miles. The county is rich in agricultural and pastoral resources and possesses advantages and capabilities which will in time make it one of the more important counties in the state. It has for its county seat the town of Pocatello, admirably situated as a future railroad centre, and is already the central trading point for a large and productive region. The Oregon Short Line and the Utah & Northern railways have their points of intersection here, and being both portions of the great Union Pacific system, the company has established here a large depot with machine shops and all the concomitants of a railroad division town. The railroad business keeps employed a large force of men, adding much to the importance and prosperity of the town.

Pocatello is located in the midst of the Bannock Indian Reservation, to the lands of which the Indian title has not yet been fully extinguished. The matter, however, is in process of adjustment by the Federal Government and the Indians, who will soon be induced to select individual tracts of land in severalty, after which set the reservation will be thrown open to settlement and the remainder of this land appropriated by white settlers. In the meantime, the town has title under the government to the townsite tract, which is of ample size for present needs.

The new county of Fremont lies north of the present county of Bingham, with an area of about 6,000 square miles, extending northward to the Montana line and to the line of the National Park. The county is well watered and possesses a wealth of resources in agricultural and grazing lands and in its forests of the finest timber. The agricultural area is settled by an industrious and thrifty population, which has accomplished wonders in the way of improvements in a section of country remote from railroads and very much isolated. The time cannot be far distant when a line of railroad will connect the Utah & Northern with the branch from the Northern Pacific, which already penetrates the National Park. The road when built will pass through the central and richest portion of Fremont County. The arable lands of this county have first and easiest access to the inexhaustible supply of water in Snake River. The people have already inaugurated a system of irrigation, much of which is in successful operation and carrying the water over a large and productive area of fertile land. When the system is completed there will not be an acre of available land in the county that will not yield its full quota to the general prosperity. The county, by its admirable position, its rich and varied resources and its proximity to the great National Park, is destined to be one of the most interesting counties in the state.

CUSTER COUNTY.

To give a full and complete description of Custer County, its resources, attractions for the settler, the mining man and the seeker of sport, health and recreation, would require a book of considerable magnitude. Hence, in an article for a pamphlet, or limited book publication, it is necessary that concentration, or "boiling down," be kept constantly in mind. This county, situated well in the central portion of the state east and west, is one of the largest of Idaho's great counties. It possesses many natural advantages and favorable inducements to permanent settlement, and is capable of sustaining a large and thrifty population. Comprising many rich mineral belts and mining districts in its topography, it is also highly favored in the distribution and extent of its fine agricultural and grazing domains. From the valleys of the Salmon and Pahsamari on the east, to the Upper Salmon, Bear and Cape Horn valleys on the west, the distance is about 125 miles; and about the same distance north and south from Prairie Basin, at the Lemhi line, to the line of Alturas on Big Lost River at the south.

Custer was first settled when it was yet a part of Lemhi and Alturas, in the early days of placer or bar and gulch mining. A few years later came the discoveries of rich gold and silver quartz, about 1876. Following this a new immigration set in; since which time the whole country has been explored, many mining towns and camps have sprung up, and the farmer and stockman have followed in the footprints of the seeker of the precious metals. The county is being well opened by good wagon roads, and the mountain trails are fast giving way to the more progressive means of thoroughfare. The nearest point to the county line from a railroad is at the summit, on the Salmon River and Ketchum wagon road, 12 miles northeast of Ketchum. Over this road daily stages run from Ketchum to all points in the interior of the county. The west end of the county, comprising the Upper Salmon country, Valley Creek Valley, Cape Horn, Bear Valley, Stanley Basin and the adjacent mining camp of Seafoam, Sheep Mountain, etc., is reached by a wagon road running north westerly from the railroad terminus at Ketchum.

At the last session of the Idaho Legislature an appropriation of $135,000 was made for a state wagon road, beginning in Boise County (the county adjoining Custer on the west) and extending through the counties of Custer and Lemhi to the mountain line near Gibbonsville. The state road bonds sold at a premium of 11 per cent, which gives the project a fund of nearly $150,000. The road can be easily completed this year, as it will connect with the county roads along the Salmon River in Custer and Lemhi counties. With the state road through the county, and with the present roads leading through the different valleys that connect with the roads leading to Ketchum and Blackfoot (the two railroad points), Custer County will be well developed so far as good road communication is concerned.

The principal valleys of the county comprise the Upper Salmon Valley, at base of Sawtooth Mountains; Cape Horn Valley and the valley of Valley Creek in the western portion of the county, as yet principally devoted to grazing purposes; the farming valleys and districts of the Middle Salmon and Round Valley, East Fork of Salmon, Upper and Lower Big Lost River, Little Lost River, Pahsamari, Warm Springs Creek, Thousand Springs Valley, Antelope Valley and some others. Adjacent to the farming districts are vast stock ranges, generally favorable to winter herding. There are numerous bands and herds of cattle, horses and sheep on the bunch-grass and white sage ranges; and the business of cattle, horse and sheep culture is an industry that is always considered safe and profitable. A very large proportion of the county revenue is derived from this source. The valleys generally range in extent from 10 to 50 miles in length and 3 to 10 miles in width. Where irrigation is necessary, the waters of rivers and mountain streams flowing into or through the valleys furnish all the water that is required. Custer County is probably as well supplied with living streams and lakes as any county in the state.

There are numerous mining towns, camps and districts scattered throughout the county, and for the most part are in close proximity to the farming and stock settlements. Among them are Bay Horse, Clayton, Garden Creek, Squaw Creek, Slate Creek, Thompson Creek, Railroad Ridge, Robinson Bar, Warm Springs Creek, Salmon River, Yankee Fork, Bonanza, Custer, Jordan Creek, Mount Estes, Capitan Mountain, Loon Creek, Stanley Basin, West Fork, Seafoam, Sheep Mountain, Elk Creek, Joe's Gulch, Germania Basin, Copper Basin, North Fork of Lost River, Pahsamari Mountains and the silver lead and copper districts near Houston or Big Lost River. Miners are working placer and quartz mines in various other localities. Recently more attention is being attracted to placer mining, both on river bars and in gulches, and the yield of gold dust is increasing annually, and will continue to increase, as many new mines of this character are being opened. In all, over 2,000 mining claims are on record in the county.

For the reduction of ores, there are in the county eight milling and smelting plants: Bay Horse Mill and Smelter, Clayton Smelter, Houston Smelter, Cinnabar Mining Company Mill, Bonanza Mill (Washington County), General Custer Mill at Custer, Fourth of July Mill on Mount Custer, and a concentrator on the Mountain King Mine at Sheep Mountain. The yield of the precious metals in the county since quartz mining became a fixed business (about thirteen years) has usually been from $1,000,000 to $1,500,000 per annum, with possibly $2,000,000 during a period of two or three years. A considerable amount of very high-grade custom ores is shipped to Omaha and other points during the summer seasons. The yearly output of the mines and mills of the county would be largely increased were it not for the protracted depression in the silver market, which has been the immediate cause of some of our heretofore most productive mines being closed to await action on the question of silver remonetization. A like influence has affected the farming communities that depend upon the prosperity of the mining camps for profitable disposal of their products.

In the Idaho Mineral Exhibit can be seen samples of ores from many of the gold, silver, copper and lead mines of Custer County.

The population of Custer County ranges from 2,500 to 3,000. The school districts number 12, with an average daily attendance of about 30, or 360 scholars of school age in the county.

The principal towns are Challis (county seat), Bay Horse, Clayton, Custer, Bonanza, Houston and Crystal. Challis, the county seat, is situated in Round Valley, about 65 miles from Ketchum, the nearest railroad point, and 130 from Blackfoot. The population is about 500. It is a point of more than ordinary importance, being centrally located and beautifully situated near the Salmon River, and is a convenient supply point for the county.

The towns and mining camps of the county have all the educational and religious privileges that are to be found in old settled communities. Some attention has of late years been given to fruit culture in the county, more particularly at Challis. Experiment has demonstrated that all the hardy berries and fruits can be cultivated successfully in any of the valleys and adjacent uplands. Some fine samples of Custer County fruits may be seen in the Idaho Fruit Exhibit, raised at an altitude of 5,000 feet to 5,500 feet. All of the mountain ranges and foothills are bountifully supplied with timber of the various pine species. Coal has been found at different points in the county, but as yet has not been successfully mined.

Custer County cannot be surpassed in its numerous summer resorts and sporting grounds. It abounds in trout streams and lakes; and large mountain game, such as deer, sheep, bear and elk, is common everywhere. The Redfish Lakes, near the Sawtooth Mountains, in the west end of the county, have long since been a favorite summer and fall resort for tourists during the "outing" season. The lakes contain both redfish and trout, and the adjacent woods furnish pleasant camping grounds. The revenues of the county are sufficient for the expenses, and county warrants command almost their face value.

CASSIA COUNTY.

The area embraced within the present boundaries of Cassia County originally formed a part of the large county of Owyhee. The county faces Snake River on the north, with a river frontage of 100 miles, and extends southward 50 miles to the northern boundary of the State of Nevada. On the west lies the present county of Owyhee, Oneida County forming the eastern boundary. The entire absence of railroad communication has retarded the progress of settlement and improvement; but notwithstanding this drawback and its isolated condition, Cassia makes a very fair showing among her more favored sisters in the state. The county has an area approaching 10,000 square miles, with a population of about 5,000. Her resources are stock raising, mining and agriculture. With her 100 miles of river frontage she has some of the best placer

IDAHO=THE GEM OF THE MOUNTAINS.

mines on Snake River. It was here that placer mining on that stream was first prosecuted on a large scale, and it is here that the best results from that industry have been obtained. Within the past few years some very valuable discoveries have been made of gold and silver bearing ledges, but as capital has not yet come to the aid of her miners, and as the means of transportation are very inadequate, these mines have not yet been sufficiently tested to make them a resource for which much can be claimed. Of patented, improved and cultivated lands the county has about 50,000 acres with an assessed valuation of $475,000. The unpatented lands which are occupied by settlers, and which have been improved to some extent, give a nearly equal acreage. The county is fairly well watered by numerous streams flowing from the mountain range on the north, and these streams have been fully utilized by local systems of irrigation. Wherever cultivated, the soil has proved fertile. The yield in hay, grain and vegetables has been fully as large per acre as that of the best and longest cultivated lands in the state. Many thousand acres of the best land lie contiguous to Snake River. A large canal, now in process of construction, takes the water from the river at a point near Idaho Falls and will, in the early future, bring an ample supply of water for all the needs of irrigation in all the lands of the county not yet provided for. By far the greater part of the large area of the county may be classed as pastoral lands, fully equal in every respect to the fine summer and winter ranges in Owyhee County. Upon these fine natural pastures, 15,000 head of cattle and about 10,000 head of horses, besides immense flocks of sheep, are kept, with but little trouble to the stockman and herder. The total assessed valuation of all the live stock within the county falls but little short of $1,000,000.

Like most of the other counties of Idaho, Cassia contains minor metals and mineral substances of many kinds, among which may be enumerated deposits of the very best fireproof mineral paint, large quarries of excellent marble, sand stone, granite, mica and many indications of coal. Of these the marble deserves especial mention. This is found in large bodies in several localities of the county, and much of the marble is of the very best quality, comparing most favorably with that found in any section of the United States. These quarries being situated in an isolated district, remote from lines of communication, are not generally known and utilized.

In his report of 1890, Governor Shoup says: "In spite of all obstacles, the industrious people of Cassia have prospered. The towns of Albion and Oakley are handsomely located and creditably built. The county affairs are economically administered. The exports of this county, though exchanged under most unfavorable conditions, are quite large. The climate is moderate and healthful. New settlers will find good locations and a fair water supply awaiting developments; they will find peace-loving communities, and public sentiment growing in intelligence and enterprise."

CANYON COUNTY.

This county is situated in the southwestern portion of the state, and until recently was a part of Ada County. It embraces some 38 townships of land, which range in altitude from 2,000 to 3,000 feet above tidewater. Probably 500,000 acres of this area may be classed as fruit and farming land (scarcely more than one-eighth of which is yet under cultivation), the remainder being grazing and mineral land. The climate of this region is one of its greatest charms, and we will refer the interested reader to the special article on climate.

In addition to a magnificent climate, the county possesses a soil so diversified, fertile and durable, and a water supply so ample for all vegetation, as to make it beyond question one of the most desirable agricultural and horticultural regions in the world. Nearly every farm and vegetable crop and deciduous fruit of the temperate zone can be grown, of excellent quality and in the greatest abundance. The county is likewise admirably adapted to special lines of husbandry, live-stock raising, both for the shambles and fancy market, dairying, bee-keeping and poultry culture. It is also within the comparatively limited prune, pear, hop and sugar-beet belt of the world. Phenomenal yields of various products of the soil could be cited, such as 1,000 bushels of wheat on 11 acres, 100 bushels of oats to the acre, 1,000 bushels of onions to an acre, 750 pounds from a seven-year old prune tree, 1,550 tons of alfalfa from 225 acres of grass in one season, 500 bushels of potatoes to the acre, under ordinary culture. These serve to show not the average crop, but the possibilities of the soil; and in this connection we extract from a report of the Caldwell Tribune an exhibit made at a fair held in the town a few years since: "The weights and measures were taken by reliable parties, and are given below: Tomatoes measuring 10 to 18 inches in circumference; in a bushel of onions, the smallest ear measuring 5½ inches in diameter, the largest exhibited was 21 inches in circumference; 12 pound beets were common—one measured 26 inches in circumference; field corn ears were 15 inches in length; a peach 9 inches, an apple 13½ inches, and a turnip 22½ inches in circumference; a carrot was 15 inches in length and the same in circumference; potatoes measured 15 inches long and 19½ round; a radish 28 long by 13½ inches in circumference; squash in circumference, was 5 feet 12 inches and weighed 71½ pounds; a pumpkin 6 feet 2 inches in circumference and weighed 120 pounds; one tobacco leaf exhibited measured 15 inches long by 11 inches wide." Without attempting a detailed statement of the average yield of all these crops, the assurance can be safely given that it will be sufficiently large to satisfy any reasonable anticipation.

Choice fruit, farm, hop and vegetable land can be had at from $5 to $20 per acre. The average orchard, in full bearing, pays from $100 to $300 per acre. Trees begin to bear at two and three years of age, and as from five to seven years of age are producing abundantly.

Idaho's fruit exhibit at the Columbian Exposition is an object lesson, more convincing than volumes of written matter, and places the state in the front rank of fruit-producing sections; and this industry alone offers a safe and profitable investment for thousands of people. Investigate the fruit business.

Chief among the resources of this county is its abundant water supply. This is of first importance in the arid region. The Snake, Payette and Boise rivers are among the largest in the intermountain country, and they are capable of furnishing the best irrigation system in the Nation. At present, some fifteen canals, varying in length from 10 to 50 miles, are completed, and several others are either in contemplation or under construction. These, with ample reservoirs, will furnish an unfailing water supply. Water applied to soil means more than moisture. It means certainty of crops and nearly always a constant enrichment of the land. Hence, the value of a reliable system of irrigation.

A timber belt, without a superior in the Northwest, embracing hundreds of square miles along the headwaters of the Payette and Boise rivers, furnishes the lumber that is needed for domestic and commercial purposes, thus insuring a lasting supply of this very necessary commodity. Hogs yield about 2,000 pounds to the acre annually, and of first quality. Pork, butter and cheese uniformly command high prices, and great quantities are yearly shipped in from other states, every pound of which could and should be produced at home. Sheep husbandry is proving very remunerative. An immense free range, well watered, is adjacent, upon which sheep feed a good portion of the year, and out of which fortunes are being made. A notable example of success in this line is that of Mr. Robert Noble, who, scarcely more than a dozen years ago, was working for day wages, and who to-day is the owner of some 45,000 sheep, the wool product of which in 1892 was 210,000 pounds, requiring a train of 12 cars to transport it across the continent to market. Many others have had marked success within a few years in the same business—some individuals driving as high as 30,000 lambs and wethers to the cheap corn of Nebraska and Kansas, to feed during the winter for the Eastern spring markets.

OLD MISSION, IDAHO.

Canyon County has undoubtedly either within her borders or directly tributary thereto, mineral deposits of amazing extent and richness. One hundred miles to the north is the marvelous copper, gold and silver region known as the Seven Devils. All who are informed, concede that this is destined to rival Butte and Anaconda when it is developed. Fifty miles to the south are the great De Lamar, Silver City and South Mountain mines, now the scene of unusual activity. Bordering on Snake River at the southern boundary of the county are the extensive gold mines of Southern Idaho, from which many beautiful and valuable stones are being taken. The new Willow Creek mining district, within the county, a recent discovery that promises great results, is also being developed. Aside from these, placer mining is now attracting wide attention. Much of the sand along the rivers of the county is known to be rich in fine gold, and not a few persons are making good wages with the "old rocker and burlap." But improved methods are being tested which will result in giving placer mining a strong impetus. A company of Caldwell capitalists has recently been organized for the purpose of working several thousand acres of placer ground located by them on the Payette River, and the enterprise promises large results.

Markets for much that is produced in Canyon County are found in the mining camps and cities of Idaho and Montana, and along the Oregon Short Line for several hundreds of miles. This is particularly true of fruits and vegetables. Fat sheep and cattle go to Omaha, Chicago, Portland, Ore., and the cities of Puget Sound. Fruits in car lots are marketed in Denver and farther east, for which special rates are secured. Prices for all products are usually very good.

The cost of living is quite reasonable. Breadstuffs, vegetables, fruits, fish and most other meats are rather below the average prices in the Eastern States. Groceries, dry goods, etc., are somewhat higher. Good table board costs from $4 to $6 per week. Rents for four and five roomed houses are from $8 to $12 per month. Farm hands and common laborers receive from $25 to $50 per month and board. Day wages are from $1.50 to $2 per day. Carpenters receive from $3 to $4 per day, and brick and stone masons and plasterers, about $5 per day. A man with team receives from $4 to $5 per day. School teachers command from $50 to $100 per month.

CALDWELL.

THE COUNTY SEAT OF CANYON COUNTY.

AND A CENTRE OF AGRICULTURAL ACTIVITY.

Caldwell, the county seat, has a population of some 1,500 people, and is located on the Oregon Short Line Railway, nearly midway between Salt Lake and Portland, at an altitude of 2,372 feet above sea level. Geographically it is convenient to all parts of the county, while the general topography of the surrounding country gives it a commanding position as a trade and prospective railroad and manufacturing centre. The town has large and enterprising mercantile houses and lumber and forwarding companies, some of which do a heavy jobbing and wholesale business. It also has one of the strongest national banks in the state, and a newspaper of more than local reputation. It has excellent public schools, and the new Presbyterian institution of learning, known as the College of Idaho. The church organizations represented are Baptist, Presbyterian, Methodist, Christian and Catholic. There are also flourishing lodges of Odd Fellows, Masons, Knights of Pythias and Good Templars. A prosperous home building and loan association has been of great service to the town, as has also its board of trade. Water works, free mail delivery and a telephone system, broad streets, good sidewalks, substantial business blocks and attractive residences are among the evidences of Caldwell's prosperity. Electric lights will probably be put in during 1893. The present trade of the town extends for 100 miles south, taking in the famous De Lamar, Silver City and South Mountain mining districts, and the valuable opal fields of Southern Idaho, only 20 miles distant. On the north and east the trade reaches far into the great timber, farming and mineral regions of Washington and Boise counties; while the new and most promising Willow Creek gold and silver mines of Canyon County are directly tributary, being about 20 miles distant, and with the easiest possible grades. Many points on the short line railway are also supplied by Caldwell merchants.

The things, then, that insure the permanent growth of Caldwell are: first a climate among the healthiest in the world; second, a location in the very heart of a great and peculiarly favored region, possessing a soil, irrigation system and climatic conditions that make it possible to produce all of the leading fruit staples, such as apples, pears, prunes, apricots, peaches, nectarines, cherries, quinces and small fruits of the highest quality, likewise immense farm and vegetable crops, including potatoes equal to the best in the land, hops and sugar beets; third, the great and practically inexhaustible mineral deposits, lying in nearly all directions, including the extensive placer fields that border the Boise, Snake and Payette rivers and their tributaries; fourth, the vast grazing regions at hand, exempt from blizzards and violent extremes, probably the best stock range in the intermountain country, and which is annually sending to the markets nearly 4,000,000 pounds of wool, 100,000 head of mutton sheep and an equal number of fat cattle and horses; fifth, the hundreds of square miles of magnificent timber immediately tributary, lying along the headwaters of the Payette and Boise rivers; sixth, it is surrounded by a prune-growing belt, probably not equaled in the country, and which must afford profitable employment for hundreds of families, both in producing and in preparing for the market.

The other towns of the county, which must share, to a greater or less extent, the resources of the country already described, and which possess excellent local advantages, are Payette, 15 miles northwest of the county seat, near the junction of the Payette and Snake rivers, a beautiful and prosperous town in the midst of a fine fruit and farm region, with extensive fruit and hop farms and nurseries, and a large saw mill. Washoa, a station one mile distant, an important lumber and saw-mill point. Wampa, 10 miles southeast of Caldwell, is also a flourishing and enterprising place in the centre of a rich agricultural section. Four miles north of Caldwell is the pretty and thrifty settlement of Middleton, which boasts of the only flouring mill at present in the county. Emmett, 20 miles north of the county seat, on the Payette River, is also a considerable business centre for the rich Upper Payette Valley, and promises to become important, and where are also located the extensive saw mills of one of Caldwell's large lumber firms. The other local trading points of the county are Falk's Store, on the Payette River, about midway between Emmett and Payette; Parma, on the Oregon Short Line, the same distance between Payette and Caldwell; and Bowman, 10 miles below Caldwell, on the Boise River.

When the local and continental lines of railroad already surveyed through the county shall have been constructed, and other development work shall have been prosecuted, all of which will be brought about at no distant day, the entire county will receive an impetus that will enable it to sustain a very large and prosperous population.

The things needed in Idaho are: more railroads, more capital for mining and canal development, more farmers, fruit growers, irrigators, stockmen, bee and poultry keepers, more flouring mills, creameries, cheese factories, canneries, tanneries, woolen mills, smelters and refineries. The time is ripe for a big forward movement along these lines, in this the greatest of all the great new states.

The holiday number of the Boise Statesman had this to say of Caldwell:

The town of Caldwell is now six years old. It is a leading station on the Oregon Short Line. It is the point of departure for mail and stage lines in many directions. It is the trade-distributing point for a vast area. It has a live board of trade, a bank, a building and loan association, excellent schools, well-sustained churches. We briefly state:

First—That Caldwell has a larger trade in proportion to its numerical population than any town in Idaho.

Second—That its business men look most closely after its general interests.

Third—That its growth in buildings and enterprises of a permanent character is steady and uniform.

Fourth—That the irrigating canals now approaching completion in its immediate vicinity will surround it with a cordon of rich farms, unexcelled in Idaho.

Fifth—That all its plans and every indication for the future points to stability and thrift.

The freights received by railroad at the Caldwell depot for the year ending June 30, 1889, amounted to 5,596,000 pounds. The freights forwarded during the same period were 9,229,000 pounds. The town owns a two-story brick schoolhouse, which cost $5,000 two years ago. In it is conducted an excellent graded school, by a principal and assistants of acknowledged educational ability.

The Depot Hotel is built and furnished in modern style, at a cost of nearly $10,000. The Methodist Church edifice, completed in July, 1889, cost $2,500. The Presbyterian church, built in 1888, cost nearly $3,500. The Baptist house of worship, built in 1884, cost $1,500. The Odd Fellows' building, built in 1887, contains the Stockgrowers and Traders Bank, H. D. Blatchley's book and drug store, and numerous offices. It cost fully $6,000 and is a credit to the town.

The largest building is occupied by F. R. Coffin & Bro., and M. B. Gwinn. This is 100 feet front by 120 feet deep, and cost about $20,000.

Montie B. Gwinn's wholesale and retail general store occupies 55 feet front of this mammoth structure, and is arranged with all the modern conveniences for facilitating his extensive business. Mr. Gwinn is a man of untiring activity and resource. He believes thoroughly in the motto, "Talk up your town," and while this is a good thing for Caldwell, it is also a good thing for himself. The resident partner, Sherman M. Coffin, manages the business of Frank R. Coffin & Bro. at this point. There may be another stock of hardware, agricultural implements, etc., in this territory exceeding in value the one kept at Caldwell by this firm; if so, there is not more than one, and not more than two equal it. In tasteful arrangement it has no superior.

Among the recent improvements not already mentioned may be noted the beautiful residence of M. B. Gwinn, which cost $5,000; the residence of Doctor Maxey, cost $1,500; D. L. Bodley's tenant house, $100; M. A. Robert's residence, $1,200; J. P. Johnson's residence, $1,000; Morris Style's residence, $1,000; A. J. Strickland's residence, $2,000; H. D. Blatchley's residence, $1,100; Charles Selvee's residence, $4,650. William Isom is about to build a residence at a cost of $3,000. Several of these buildings are in cottage style, and are exceedingly tasteful and handsome. The grounds attached are being ornamented, and special attention given to the cultivation of trees, grass and flowers.

As a centre of trade Caldwell attracts to the counters of its business men a large percentage of the trade of Long Valley, and of all the rich agricultural and mineral region intervening between the two localities; also, a fair portion of the trade from Payette Valley below the town of Emmett. To this may be added almost the entire trade of the lower half of the Boise Valley, and a large portion of the business coming from that section of Eastern Oregon lying contiguous to Snake River. Still another source of profitable business, belonging almost exclusively to Caldwell, is the agricultural and pastoral sections of Owyhee County lying between Snake River and the higher elevations of the Owyhee Mountains. Through the energy and enterprise, and the intelligent liberality of her business men, Caldwell lies thus far succeeded in holding and controlling her portion of the field of trade as above outlined, and there is every reason for believing that, guided and moved by the spirit that now animates her citizens, she will not only continue to hold this large and rich field but that it will grow in value to her and expand indefinitely as the years go by.

NAMPA.

The Home of Irrigation Profusely and Interestingly Illustrated.

Resources of the Rapid Growing City on Lake Ethel.

In presenting the city of Nampa to the intelligent reader of Idaho's World's Fair Souvenir, it is not the intention of the writer to portray in glowing terms the idea that this is a town of every conceivable resource. He will, however, attempt to illustrate the marvelous growth of this young but thriving town, and give, in as brief a manner as possible, the means by which it has grown to the important commercial centre it now is. It would consume too much space to detail the history of Nampa from its earliest date of settlement to the present time with its 700 population. Briefly speaking, it may truthfully be said that the old saying, that "It's the people that make the town," may be applied to the junction city that connects Boise City with the main line of the Union Pacific Railroad. The town is blessed with an enterprising and cultured class of citizens, whose every motive is to promote their little city to a high degree of prominence. To-day the business and social qualities of Nampa are superior to many towns with double her population, and every branch of her several educational and religious institutions is conducted in a commendatory manner.

It must be remembered that Nampa was not platted until the year 1887. Mr. Alexander Duffes carefully weighed the surrounding country when he made his homestead entry, as it is to-day upon what may be termed the summit of the great quantity of lands immediately tributary and affords a most pleasing view of the rich and prolific surrounding country. Several attractive structures are to be seen here, among which is the Central Public School building, which, like a veritable pyramid, overlooks beautiful Lake Ethel. Not only are the public buildings of such an importance to the splendid appearance of Nampa, but there are many residences noted for their architectural beauty. Among these may be named those of Alexander Duffes, James McGee, J. M. Jones, A. Fouch, J. Steinmetz, George Duval and F. C. Henry. A spacious and well kept hotel is under the management of a thoroughly competent person, and the banking and business blocks are occupied and extensively stocked to supply the demands of the neighboring inhabitants.

It would be hard to judge the number of acres of lands directly tributary to Nampa, but a conservative estimate would place it at 150,000 acres.

Now, the resources of this town, with such a brilliant and glorious future, may be figured in several ways, but we will consider the vast amount of arable land that lies directly tributary, and is, by the efforts of the irrigationist, being thoroughly watered, made the most productive soil to be found anywhere in the Pacific Northwest. As has often been stated, "irrigation is king" in the sagebrush districts of Idaho, and the results of its quenching capabilities are teeming orchards and thriving grain fields.

The Boise & Nampa Irrigation, Land and Lumber Company is the title of the enterprise of which Mr. J. M. Jones is the secretary, treasurer and general manager. Here a magnificent system of ditches, the total length of which is 255 miles, has been constructed, covering 200,000 acres, and a great part of the sagebrush swept out of existence. For several years past a canal known as the "Ridenbaugh Ditch" had been in operation. It was only 8 or 9 miles long, and carried but little water, which was taken from the Boise River, about 5 miles above the city of that name. The Idaho Central Canal and Land Company purchased this canal, who in turn disposed of it to the present owners at a large figure, the men who organized the Boise & Nampa Irrigation Land and Lumber Company. This latter company was stocked for $1,000,000. The officers elected are H. E. Simmons, formerly vice president of the American Investment Company; president James A. McGee, of Nampa, vice president; J. M. Jones, secretary, treasurer and general manager, and R. W. Purdum, one of the first residents of the town, assistant manager. Having arranged the details of organization and preliminary work, these men of energy set about placing their bonds. This was readily accomplished through the American Investment Company, the bonds being marketed both in the East and in foreign countries. With the proceeds made available by the sale of the bonds this company set about its work of construction and land reclamation. The work was pushed energetically and to-day this section of the country possesses one of the best systems of irrigation west of the Great Divide.

Of the canal system managed at Nampa, a writer says that the country through which the canal runs is one of magnificent formation for artificial reservoirs and lakes, of which there will be ten, all very near the city.

The work of canal construction in this section has been revolutionized. By the use of their new ditcher the company has opened up laterals at the rate of from three to five miles per day. The cost of ditching a section of land is about $100, according to the company's figures, this being remarkably

low. In fact the attention of many Eastern financiers has been attracted to the enterprise, just on account of the cheapness of construction when compared with the possibilities of profitable returns. This enterprise possesses one feature which makes it exceedingly valuable, and that is the facility and cheapness with which it can furnish power of all kinds, either for the farmer or for any kind of manufacturing industry. From the point of diversion on the Boise to the city of Nampa there is a fall of 396 feet, and 165 feet from the second lake. Thus it will be noticed that the city possesses ample water supply for water works, fire protection and for mills and work shops innumerable. And then, after turning the wheels of industry, the life-giving water goes to the soil, where it fertilizes countless acres, and adds to the agricultural prosperity of the country.

One hears nothing but words of commendation concerning the business propositions of the company. The farmers have been dealt with most liberally and every effort has been made to aid them in the work of reclamation and town building. The cost of water is $1.50 per acre per year, or $12.50 per acre for perpetual water rights, with a nominal fee to assist in the maintenance. It costs but $5 per acre to clear off the sagebrush, and when once cleared the ground is susceptible of easy cultivation. The soil is exceedingly rich, containing all of the elements necessary to plant life. It is decomposed lava and well adapted to all the cereals, clover, timothy and alfalfa. The fruits of the temperate zone yield in abundance. Apples, pears, peaches, plums, strawberries and watermelons have been grown with magnificent success. The company will set out extensive orchards and sow vast tracts of grain during the coming season. With an example thus set before them, the farmers of the beautiful Boise and Snake valleys will be stimulated to renewed efforts. The year recently closed has been a successful one in many respects for this new enterprise. Water has been furnished to prove up 8,000 acres; every legal subdivision of 4,000 acres more have been ditched, and applications have been received for perpetual water rights for 10,000

Of the country tributary to Nampa, a writer says: The town of Nampa, situated on the Oregon Short Line Railroad, 20 miles southwest of Boise City and 9 miles east of Caldwell, though numbering only a few years of existence and a few hundred inhabitants, gives certain promise of rapid growth in the early future. It is surrounded on all sides by a wide expanse of the most fertile and productive lands on the continent. The number of acres of this choice land that will be directly tributary to it—at its very doors, so to speak—may be safely estimated at 500,000. The only thing that has retarded the growth of the town is the lack of water, and this want will soon be supplied by the irrigating canals, now in process of rapid construction. When these canals reach Nampa, an event that cannot possibly be deferred more than a few months at the farthest, a new era of growth and prosperity will dawn upon the town, and it will move forward with the strength and the strides of a young giant. Besides the extensive era of fertile lands which Nampa can claim as her own, she will continue to be a successful competitor for a large share of the trade of the Boise Valley, as well as for that of the agricultural sections of Owyhee county. The agricultural resources of the town alone will suffice to justify the prediction that within five years Nampa will have a large population. But agriculture is only one of the many rich resources of this young and promising town. The completion of the canals to, through and below Nampa will afford many admirable sites for the erection of machinery for varied manufacturing purposes. One of these sites, and probably the best on the lines of the canals, is in close contact with the present builded portion of the townsite. Here a fall of several feet can be secured, quite sufficient to make the water of the canals available for any and all purposes desired.

Another large and permanent element of growth is found in the immense stock ranges of Owyhee county—a vast region which will continue to be utilized for stock-raising purposes. Nampa can justly lay claim, as she is already enjoying, a very large percentage of the trade coming from the shipping of cattle and other stock to Eastern and Western markets. Of this large trade, the portion which Nampa can claim as exclusively hers is found in the herds of fattest beef cattle and other food stock that will be furnished by the great army of farmers occupying the land directly tributary to the town.

It is no wild conjecture to say that Nampa is destined to be a railroad centre, and the natural receiving and distributing point for the extensive region of which she is the centre. True it is, that no one can name or locate the railroads of the future, or predict with any certainty the changes that the years may bring in railroad matters. But Nampa is already an important point on the Oregon Short Line and the point of junction with the Idaho Central. It is as certain as any future event can be, that the Idaho Central will have extension, both east and west. These two roads alone will suffice to place Nampa on an equal footing, in point of railroad facilities and advantages, with any other town in the State of Idaho.

Nampa occupies a commanding position in the great, natural pathway of all the railroads that will in the future be built to connect the upper half of the Mississippi Valley with the great West; and her chances of being touched by all of these is equal to those of any other town on the Oregon Short Line.

In point of beauty of situation and salubrity of climate, no locality in the great intermountain region can claim precedence over Nampa. For picturesque, romantic and varied scenery, combining every feature that can please the eye and delight the heart, there is no spot that can surpass the picture which Nampa will present after a few years of cultivation shall have converted her broad and fertile plains into productive fields, meadows and orchards.

Of the intelligent foresight, energy and enterprise of her citizens Nampa has no need to boast. Their work and their genuine staying qualities show for themselves, and are a certain guarantee of her bright and prosperous future.

PUBLIC SCHOOL AND OTHER BUILDINGS IN NAMPA

GLIMPSES OF NAMPA ACROSS LAKE ETHEL.

INDIAN SCHOOL AT FORT LAPWAI.

MOSCOW, IDAHO

VIEW OF THE GREAT DE LAMAR MINE.

ELMORE COUNTY.

This county once formed a part of the original county of Alturas, which has since been carved into the counties of Alturas, Elmore and Logan. The first settlements made, and the first mining enterprises prosecuted, within the region now covered by these three counties were in what is now Elmore County. Mines were discovered and worked here as early as the summer of 1863. The northern portion of the county is a mountainous region, drained by the North and South Boise rivers and their tributaries. These mountains are high and rugged, and covered for the most part with a dense forest growth, affording almost inexhaustible supplies of the finest timber. The mining towns of Rocky Bar and Atlanta are situated in this mountain section, and it was around these as centres that the first mines were discovered and worked. During the earlier period of mining operations the output of the precious metals was very considerable. The mines are to-day as good as ever, many of them better, but a variety of causes have combined to make mining in this section less ardently pursued than it was in former years. The discovery of rich galena deposits in the Wood River country and other discoveries and mining excitements drew off a very large portion of the mining population, and the same causes, together with the fact that this mining section is quite isolated, difficult of access and remote from the lines of transportation, have prevented the attention of miners from being attracted to the field thus partially deserted. Lately, however, the interest in mining is beginning to revive with the certainty of approaching railroads and the general rapid increase of population in the state. There are good reasons for the hope that a railroad will traverse this mountain region within two years at the furthest. When this is realized, mining operations will be revived on a large scale, and even lumber making will set in, and the vast wealth of mine and forest that has so long been dormant will give this portion of the county the prominence to which it is entitled.

Southward of the mountain section and extending to Snake River, we have more than one-half of the entire area of the county composed of fertile land, much of which has already been reclaimed and cultivated, though there are several hundreds of thousands of acres of choice land for which irrigation has not yet been provided. The available water supply will eventually prove sufficient for this, but the capital for the construction of canals is thus far wanting. The total assessed valuation of property in the county approximates $1,250,000. Of this the valuation of 17,000 acres of improved, patented lands is about $90,000, and the valuation of 5,000 head of stock cattle and 2,000 head of horses aggregates about $120,000.

The growth of Elmore County has not been so rapid as that of some other counties in the state, but it is quite satisfactory, all things considered. The area of the county is a little less than 6,000 square miles, while but a small percentage of this area can be justly called worthless. The county, taken as a whole, is very rich in natural resources, and her people can well afford to bide their time for the growth and development that are certain to come with the general advance of the county.

MOUNTAIN HOME.

The Commercial Centre and County Seat of Elmore County.

It is usually found that the seat of a county government is the centre of trade and, therefore, it naturally grows to be the chief city of the district embodied in the county in which it is located. Situated upon the Union Pacific Railway, about 512 miles from Portland, Ore., may be found an enterprising and rapidly growing city, which is no exception to this rule.

With an increasing population of about 500 persons, Mountain Home, the county seat of Elmore County, Idaho, lies in one of the most productive agricultural and horticultural regions known in the irrigated districts of Idaho.

As has been fully demonstrated in this work relative to irrigation, all that is needed to make the great sagebrush deserts of Idaho the most prolific and lucrative agricultural spots in the Northwest is the building of ditches and reservoirs to utilize the abundance of water that the ever-quenching streams of Southern Idaho have at the disposal of the irrigationist or farmer.

The county seat of Elmore County takes great pride in publishing the fact that within her immediate vicinity every advantage is being taken of what Nature alone has done to water the thirsty sagebrush district in which she is located, and that there is to-day a complete reservoir system in operation at and near this point. It must also be stated that there is in course of erection at Mountain Home a reservoir that will have a capacity that will excel any similar construction in the State of Idaho.

Immense capital has been invested in the industry which alone would push Mountain Home to a front rank in the lines of commercial centres. These enormous investments are none other than promoting the irrigation of the unwatered lands.

It must be understood, however, that this section is not void of former cultivation, for to-day there may be found thrifty fields of superior grain and teeming orchards of excellent fruit trees, all bearing in a most advantageous manner.

Besides being the distributing point of so rich an agricultural section, Mountain Home claims the honor of stating that the largest output of wool in the State of Idaho is registered at her warehouses, the shipment this year having already reached 1,000,000 pounds. A rival town would look upon this statement with envy, but jealousy would necessarily cease when the entire live-stock industry of Mountain Home Valley is considered. Immense quantities of horses, cattle and sheep are shipped from this point yearly.

Daily stages traverse the remote sections of Elmore County, which include the rich mineral and forest districts. Daily communication is made with Rocky Bar and Pine Tree and tri-weekly stages make trips to Atlanta, Grand View, Castle Creek and Oneida. In this way it will be seen that Mountain Home is the supply point of a vast belt of country with diversified resources.

The city of Mountain Home is most beautifully located on what was once nothing but a sea of bunch grass. Imbued with an unusual spirit of enterprise, her citizens have aided and caused to be built a most home-like, consequently comfortable, and attractive town. It is well platted, with broad and level streets bordered on either side with beautiful shade trees and well-built sidewalks. The religious and educational facilities are in keeping with those of Eastern towns and her municipal government is in the hands of citizens who are loyal to the little city they represent. The different lines of mercantile business are well represented, and the volume of exchange is of a character that speaks loudly for the prolific district that lies tributary to her gates. An ably-edited and well-circulated newspaper goes forth weekly and expounds to the world, in a clear, authentic and concise manner, the news of general interest which is afforded in the busy section of this city.

Information as to every branch of industry that may be applied within the section in or about Mountain Home will be promptly rendered upon application to the Board of Trade

IDAHO COUNTY.

Idaho is the largest county in the State of Idaho and one of the largest in the United States. It occupies the heart of Idaho and extends from Oregon on the west to Montana on the east. Its western base is washed by the waters of Snake River, and it is bounded on the east by the Bitter Root Mountains, a distance of nearly 200 miles. From north to south it covers an even greater distance. Through the centre of this great area Salmon River and its multitudinous tributaries drain the largest and least known scope of mineral country on the Pacific Slope. Through its northern limits flows the noble Clearwater, the largest affluent of Snake River, draining on the west slope of the Bitter Root Divide the finest forests of yellow pine, tamarack, red fir and cedar on the continent. Throughout the region drained by these streams are vast areas of unexplored country, whose surrounding characteristics indicate extensive mineral zones containing large deposits of the royal metals. In Idaho County is situated the great Camas Prairie. Ex-Governor Stevenson, in his report to the Secretary of the Interior for 1888, speaking of this region, said: "Being perfectly familiar with the great Northwest, I have no hesitation in saying no other locality offers more or better inducements to the homeseeker than this county. The people are enterprising, intelligent and progressive. A complete system of road and school districts is in operation, and the fine farms, buildings, orchards and other improvements on every side tell the traveler that this is the home of a happy, prosperous and thriving people." Of this great Camas Prairie it can justly be said that the Almighty never planned so big a piece of country with less waste land. It is a part of the great Clearwater Basin, which the Nez Perce Indians have so long monopolized as their reservation. Its peculiar situation between the mountains secures plenty of natural rainfall; consequently, irrigation is not required. Grain, hay, vegetables and fruit are here grown to the greatest perfection and with comparatively little expense. The drawback these people have to contend with is to find a market for their products, as there is not a mile of railroad in the county at present. Millions of bushels of wheat could be grown for export, but as producers have to freight by team 60 miles to Lewiston, the head of navigation on Snake River, they content themselves with raising only sufficient of the cereals to supply a home market at the mining camps in the surrounding mountains. Owing to the absence of an outside market for their products the residents of Camas Prairie are largely engaged in stock raising, and the pursuit of agriculture is a secondary consideration. Nearly everybody has cattle, horses and hogs to sell and the sales of live stock aggregate $80,000 annually. The Prairie, the adjoining Indian reservation, the river canyons and the vacant lands not yet taken up, all combine to make the Camas Prairie portion of Idaho County a paradise for the professional stockgrower, for here is found a combination of the finest bunch-grass range, with abundant water and a milder climate than any other locality possesses. Stock growing is, indeed, the principal industry of Idaho County, and very nearly one-half of its taxable property is found in its herds of live stock. There is more diversified farming here than in any other county in the state, and this perhaps accounts for the prosperity of its inhabitants. Thus it will be seen that every element of prosperity lies at the doorstep of every man who has the good fortune to acquire title to a tract of the fertile soil of Camas Prairie. Tickle it with a plow and it will laugh you a harvest of flour. Camas Prairie must necessarily be the supply point for a tributary mineral and lumbering region for a distance of 150 miles.

Although growing in importance slowly, owing chiefly to her great distance from the settled portions of the country, the difficulty of access, the fear of Indians and the little that is known of her resources, it is not hard to perceive that Idaho is a county of great value, and that great as the changes have been in the last ten years, they will be still greater in the next, viewing the prospect for more rapid growth in the light of the character of population, the facilities for reaching the county which the railroad companies are now providing, and the flood of light which has recently shone upon her resources. In point of fact Idaho County has a greater diversity of resources than any other county in the state, and her products are beginning to excite the attention of the country and awakening it to the conviction that it has productive capabilities not heretofore suspected. The business of farming commenced in Camas Prairie nearly thirty years ago, and in all that time there has never been a total failure of crops. There is, therefore, no point of this beautiful and glorious section that has not its fertility and values thoroughly established. With the enjoyment of ample and regular railroad transportation assured in the near future, nothing is now wanted but people to occupy Camas Prairie fully — an active, enterprising, sagacious people, who will appreciate, utilize, extend and increase the blessings they enjoy.

The population of Idaho County, according to the census of 1890, was 2,955. Since then, however, it has more than doubled. Its property valuation is about $1,250,000. It has 25 school districts, with 1,011 school children, and in 1891 we expended $9,869.05 of county revenue for educational purposes.

But great as the agricultural possibilities of Idaho County are, the most important factor in its growth and development will be the production of its mines. These not only furnish work for our own people, but for men from other counties, and thus make a profitable home market for the products of our farm lands. Having such mines practically in our midst has been the means of placing labor and wealth in the hands of all, and it is an industry that must necessarily increase in the immediate future. The Clearwater country has been aptly termed the "Mother of Gold," because the discoveries which led to the first settlement of the country in 1860 were the wonderfully rich placer fields of Pierce City, Oro Fino, Elk City, Florence, Warrens and the rich bars of the Clearwater River, from which millions of dollars of gold were extracted, and whose product to-day places Idaho County second in the list of gold-producing counties in the state. The product of our placer fields will hereafter be enormously increased through the operations of capitalists who are opening up the flat placer ground by dredge and other improved systems which were beyond the reach of individuals.

The quartz and placer mines of Warrens district on the south side of Salmon River, always good, are now producing better than ever, owing to the construction by the state of a wagon road into the camp from the north and south, thus permitting the introduction of heavy machinery and reducing the high freight tariff which the miners have had to pay for thirty years on every necessary of life. Warrens is an important camp, and its prospects of growth and new development were never so bright as at this moment. It produces the richest gold quartz ever found in Idaho, and mining operators will find it a most inviting field.

But the future great gold camp of Idaho County, and, indeed, of all Idaho, is in Elk City district. The quartz ledges of this camp are exclusively gold bearing and vary in size from 1 foot to 30 feet in width. The ore will average in value from $8 to $20 per ton. A vast amount of development work is being done, but the owners being principally poor men, there are not many developed properties in the district at present. The Buster, near Elk City, and the Cleveland, on Relief Creek, 10 miles south, are the only claims developed to any depth, and they show up handsome veins of ore of very uniform quality. Mineralogically, the ores of the camp consist of a quartz gangue, carrying free gold and iron pyrites. Quartz is a characteristic matrix, though other matrices occur. They are universally concentrating ores.

The ores of Elk City are called "low grade" in this county, but in California they would be termed high-grade ores. The Idaho Mine, of Grass Valley, is worked to a depth of 2,000 feet on ore that averages $6 per ton. This mine has yielded $11,000,000 in gold and paid $5,000,000 in dividends. In Sierra County the Sierra Buttes Mine has yielded $8,000,000, and is worked to a depth of 3,000 feet, with not an ounce of ore exceeding $7 per ton in value. The character of these ores is identical with those of Elk City, and the process of reduction is the same, viz: milling and concentrating.

The state has now under construction a wagon road from Grangeville to Elk City, a distance of 50 miles, to cost $8,000, which will prove of great value to the camp. Investors seeking gold propositions will do well to investigate the mines of Elk City district in Idaho County.

The principal town in Idaho County is Grangeville, in the heart of Camas Prairie. It is a farmer's, miner's, stockman's and prospector's trading point, and does a very large mountain trade, as well as supplying the smaller stores all over the county. The town was established in 1874, and has a population of 850 souls. Among its social organizations are a Methodist academy, Methodist and Episcopal churches with resident ministers, a brass band, choir and orchestra, Odd Fellows', Masonic and Patrons of Husbandry lodges, a strong military company, a Chautauqua circle, a public graded school system and other indications of culture and refinement not usually found in so isolated a community. The town is building up with great rapidity, and the prospect of railroad connections in the next few months, together with the building of the state wagon road system connecting it with the mining camps to the north, east and south, as well as the opening of the adjoining Nez Perce Indian Reservation of 545,000 acres of additional tributary farming lands, all conspire to place it in position to speedily become one of the most important towns in the state. All the manufacturing, banking, express and commercial business of this great county is transacted in Grangeville. Wood and lumber is obtained from the timber belt two miles south of the town. Water is found at six to twenty feet. A new schoolhouse has been built, its population, wealth and business is rapidly increasing, and the formation of a new social and commercial world is being moulded into form. The State Agricultural Experiment Station is located here, and the citizens are strongly exerting themselves to secure the location of the State Agricultural College, the Soldiers' Home and State Normal School. Deposits of lime, granite and other building materials are close at hand. Quartz and placer mines are being developed within ten miles of the town. Several saw and planing mills are being operated in the near vicinity, and every adjunct in the way of natural resources and public spirit and enterprise exist. Grangeville is a rising town, and, in the slang of the day, a good town to keep your eye on.

KOOTENAI COUNTY.

Occupying the extreme northern portion of the State of Idaho and forming by its peculiar shape what is known as the Idaho "Panhandle," Kootenai County presents an approximate area of 15,000 square miles, with a surface so diversified, so replete with grand and interesting natural features, so richly endowed with varied and inexhaustible resources and with all the favoring conditions and advantages, that to those who know this charming and attractive region it is one of the many wonders and surprises encountered here in the great and golden West that a section of country like this should still be so partially known and so little appreciated. Good water, rich mines, fine timber, great water power, temperate climate and the best agricultural land are the characteristics of this county; yet few Eastern people are aware that a region so favored exists in the far away Northwest. Large mountain areas, covered with the usual forest trees found in this latitude, furnish sources for fuel and lumber sufficient for the needs of all future generations. There are three beautiful lakes, Pend d'Oreille, Cœur d'Alene and a host of others of minor size, all filled with delicious trout and surrounded by towering mountains, in whose cool and shady recesses the hunter will find every description of wild game, from the elk and caribou to the chattering pine squirrel. Brooks of sparkling cool water fed by perennial springs go babbling down the mountain sides to join their sister streamlets on their way to the great river of the West. There is no more healthful region in Idaho. Warmed and made genial by the kindly ocean current that sweeps along the western Pacific Coast, the balmy air is forced, by the western winds that prevail during the winter, up and along the Columbia and its tributaries and diffused throughout the interior, its effects being everywhere felt, giving a winter climate to this high northern latitude that is entirely beyond the comprehension and belief of the shivering citizens of localities on the same parallel east of the Rocky Mountain chain. Thus the winter climate of Kootenai County is as mild as that of any other portion of climate-favored Idaho excepting the valleys of the great rivers, where a much lower altitude compels a slight difference; while the summer climate is what is everywhere found among the Idaho mountains, where forest shades and cool and refreshing streams temper the summer heat to a degree that makes mere existence a delight. Here in this favored region, streams, lakes and mountains combine to make natural scenery of unrivaled beauty and loveliness. Sites for homes, where every natural feature and condition for pleasure and comfort abound, are open alike to rich and poor.

The mines of Kootenai County form, virtually, as yet an unopen storehouse of boundless wealth. The great wealth of the Cœur d'Alene mines and those of other sections of the state and the large mining operations in the better known mining sections have prevented any considerable attention being given to a region equally rich in the precious metals and quite equal in the extent of its mineral deposits to that of any other section. In Kootenai County there is a great quartz belt, the like of which the world has never seen. This great belt crops out at irregular intervals across the entire length of the mountain area and extends into the British possessions. It appears in the Weber group, Jumbo, Eagle and other properties around Chloride and the Homestake in the Granite district. There it disappears beneath Pend d'Oreille Lake and crops out again six miles north of Hope. Next we find it on the Yak, and from there it goes on, grander, stronger, richer, until it reaches the big silver leads of the Kootenai Mining and Smelting Company.

The agricultural resources of the county can be best judged by the amount of land owned, cultivated and improved. The lack of reliable statistics makes it impossible to give this with entire accuracy, but the number of acres now occupied and cultivated cannot be much short of 200,000 acres. This county has a broad area of fertile prairie land in one continuous body, besides numerous valleys along the streams which drain the more mountainous portion. The agricultural products embrace all the cereals and vegetables grown elsewhere in Idaho. Fruit trees of many varieties also grow luxuriously and bear abundantly. The northern portion of the county is traversed by the Northern Pacific and the Great Northern railways. These two great transcontinental thoroughfares, with the branches and feeders which the growth of the country will necessitate, afford ample facilities for travel and transportation.

The present population of Kootenai County may be stated approximately at 6,000, and its assessed valuation of property at $3,200,000.

As a summary of the resources and advantages of this county, here is what Governor Shoup says in his report of 1890: "The county is attracting attention for many reasons. First is the diversity of its resources. Its forests will furnish employment for men and money for the next hundred years. It has a larger variety of timber than other counties of Idaho, and will become the seat of manufactures on a large scale. Its climate and soil facilitate agricultural productions of the greatest variety and abundance. It is the best watered section for hundreds of miles, as it has large lakes and broad, clear, deep rivers. Its mines are constantly increasing in value and productiveness. All the resources are combined by easy water and railway communications, facilitating exchange of productions and giving employment to all kinds of labor. Kootenai County in natural scenery cannot be excelled. Thousands of tourists find its lakes, rivers, mountains and valleys a perpetual source of health and pleasure. There is no pleasanter spot during July and August, no location better deserving the title of the 'Hunters' Paradise.'"

Kootenai is the home county of Hon. James M. Wells, Idaho's Columbian Commissioner; and while the commissioner has every reason to be proud of the county which contains his home, and which he has so long honored, Kootenai County and the entire state are also proud of its representative, who has labored so indefatigably and successfully to give Idaho her proper place in the great Columbian Exposition.

From sketches and photographs
by Mr. C. C. Clawson.

SCENERY IN CUSTER COUNTY.

No. 1—Red Fish Lake.   No. 2—Sawtooth Mountains.   No. 3—Rocks Near Bonanza.   No. 4—Natural Stone House Near Big Redfish Lake.   No. 5—Cone Mine, Sawtooth Range.   Nos. 6 and 7—Stumps of Petrified Trees.

GREAT SHOSHONE FALLS

BRIDAL VEIL FALLS.

IDAHO=THE GEM OF THE MOUNTAINS.

LOGAN COUNTY.

Logan County is centrally located and occupies an important position among the counties of Southern Idaho. This county originally formed a part of old Alturas County. It has an area of 7,000 square miles, with a population approaching 4,000. Within the eastern half of the county is embraced the interesting section known from the first white occupation of the country as the great Camas Prairie.

This section forms the most important tract of agricultural lands in Logan County. It extends east and west on either side of the Malad River a distance of 100 miles. The tillable area is 80 miles long, and has an average width of about 15 miles. Every foot of this tract is available for agriculture, and but a few years will elapse before it will all be owned and cultivated. The prairie is a high plateau at an estimated average altitude of 5,000 feet. Unlike most portions of Southern Idaho, irrigation in this district is unnecessary. Underneath the rich soil, at a depth of but a foot or two, is a substratum impervious to water, so that the water that soaks into the soil from the melting snows in the mountains remains close to the surface, affording what is called "sub-irrigation." The climate on the prairie is delightful. Snow falls about the middle of December, remaining on the ground until about the middle of March. The weather is not cold; the air being light and dry, the cold is felt but little. As soon as the snow goes off the farmer can commence plowing. The principal crops are wheat, oats, barley and hay. The average yields are: wheat, 35 bushels; oats, 60 bushels; and barley, 30 bushels per acre. The county is well adapted for the industry of stock raising. The melting snows in the spring months give abundant moisture to maintain a luxuriant growth of grass for the herds during the summer months. On the approach of winter the herds find a fine winter range along the Snake River, where rain falls during the months that the snow falls in the northern part of the county. By moving stock back and forth with the changing seasons it is kept in good condition the year round, with but little extra feeding. The number of cattle, horses and sheep now kept upon the ranges in the county will count well up toward 50,000.

The mining districts are situated in the northern portion of the county, with Bellevue, the county seat, as a centre of operations and a supply point. The mines consist of gold and silver bearing ledges, many of which have been worked sufficiently to fully demonstrate their extent and richness. Some causes have operated to bring on short suspensions and lulls in the prosecution of this industry, but a general revival of the mining interest has now set in, and the mining districts of Logan County will be certain to share in this era of prosperity. This county has been too long a profitable field for mining development to permit the slightest doubt of its mineral wealth now. Millions have been mined, and millions more will be extracted from the gold and silver ledges of Logan County. There are about 300,000 acres of excellent forest lands in the county, sufficient for fuel and lumber during several generations. More than 4,000,000 feet of lumber are annually manufactured from these forests.

Bellevue, the county seat, is the largest town in the county, and has a population of about 1,000. The town is pleasantly situated near the northern boundary of the county, with some of the finest mines in the state in the immediate vicinity, and at the gateway to the interesting Wood River country. The southern half of the county extends from the Camas Prairie section on the north to Snake River on the south, and embraces a large area of the finest sage-brush lands. These lands, of course, require irrigation to make them available for agriculture. This has been provided to a certain extent, but much yet remains to be done in this direction. The local streams can all be utilized for the purposes of irrigation, and these alone will assist in reclaiming large areas of fertile lands. The rest can all be reached by a canal from Snake River, where the water supply is inexhaustible.

The flourishing town of Shoshone is the junction of the Union Pacific Railway line and its Wood River branch. This town has already grown to be an important trading point and has a large business, derived from the growing agricultural and grazing regions that surround it.

A most interesting feature in the topography of the county is found along its frontage on Snake River, where many of the great natural wonders of that truly wonderful river are found. Among these may be mentioned the great Shoshone Falls, the Twin Falls, three miles above, and the intervening rapids and cataracts. The river winds between high perpendicular walls of basalt, offering at every turn the most magnificent pictures of wild and rugged scenery. In the neighborhood of the great falls are the Blue Lakes, a most romantic spot, framed in by towering basaltic cliffs on every side. At a point several miles below the falls, from the upper section of the cliffs that front the river on the Logan County side, great springs gush out from some, as yet unknown, source, and, deluging the sides of the cliff, collect into a large stream which finds its way into the river. Most of these grand and interesting natural features will be found illustrated in this work.

LATAH COUNTY.

When it comes to a comparison of the agricultural resources of the different counties of Idaho, Latah will be found robed in an air of independence, which is sustained by the fact that her qualifications for producing all the fruits and cereals known to the agricultural world are unequaled and unapproached. It was not so very many years ago that the immigrant would have ridiculed the idea of an attempt to cultivate and raise agricultural products upon the bunch-grass hills of the Palouse and Potlatch districts. But within the few years that have been devoted to farming in that region, the fact has been demonstrated that not a country in the world can compete with the enormous yield of grain that has been placed upon record in the statistical houses of not only the United States, but of the entire world. It is not necessary to stipulate that Latah County is fortunately blessed with unlimited resources, but that which she begs to have said is, that she leads all in the yield of wheat. As before stated, Latah County embraces part of the famous Palouse and Potlatch wheat belts. Here the soil is of a deep black loam and Nature serves this favored spot with all the moisture necessary to the growing of crops. The attention of the farmers is given to the growing of wheat, oats, barley, rye, flax and all the fruits which orchardists usually cultivate for a profit. Fruit growing, however, is yet in its infancy, as the farmer has never given his attention to that industry owing to the immense income derived from wheat production. Latah County takes great pleasure in stating that it was in this vicinity that 301 bushels of wheat was raised and harvested upon an acre of ground. It will be very hard for our Eastern friends to believe this, but affidavits may be seen to that effect upon application to any interested person living in the neighborhood of Latah. Residents of the old Eastern states will also wonder in astonishment when they are told that some of the land in this section will and does bring as much money per acre as do the improved and cultivated farms of New England. It may clearly be seen why the land is so valuable. Wheat will average in the neighborhood of from 35 to 60 bushels per acre, and the price is seldom below 60 cents per bushel; so it will be seen that it pays to invest in land that has never been known to fail in giving the farmer a good crop. Such a thing as a failure of a crop in the Palouse and Potlatch country is unknown, and the cultivator is always sure of a fair yield. The area of Latah County is 1,100 square miles, of which at least three-fourths is available for farming purposes. The wheat yield of the county has reached in the neighborhood of 1,000,000 bushels, and when the entire county is placed under cultivation, it is safe to say that the production of wheat in this county will exceed that of the present yield of the entire state. In his report of 1890, Governor Shoup says: "The rapid growth of this most prosperous county is shown by comparing the assessment returns of 1889 and 1890. The total assessed value of property of the county in 1889 was $1,203,192; in 1890 it is given as above $2,771,143. This is an increase of 130.3 per cent in one year, a growth not equaled by any county in the state, and it is possible, not equaled by any important county in the United States."

Another of Latah's lucrative resources is her timber. Here may be found beautiful specimens of pine, fir, spruce, tamarack and cedar. The timber is cut to a great extent, the annual output reaching in the neighborhood of 20,000,000 feet of lumber. The county does not pose as a mineral-bearing district, but it is within her boundaries that is mined the opal that has given the section such a widely known reputation. The specimens from these opal mines are superior to most any others that have heretofore been exhibited by other countries. Soft coal undoubtedly lies in the region covered by Latah County, and the famous Muscovite mica mine cannot be placed second to any of its kind.

There are several good towns in Latah County, of which Moscow is the larger, and as to population, it will rival Boise City very closely. It is here that the State University is located, and the imposing structures that adorn the broad and level streets of Moscow would be a credit to a city of ten times the size. A page illustration in this number will portray an idea of the appearance of the business centre of the metropolis and clearly set forth the validity of Latah's capital.

While stock raising is not looked upon as a principal industry in Latah County, cattle and horses receive a great deal of attention by the residents. They have given much time and care to the raising of blooded stock, particularly horses.

LEMHI COUNTY.

Lemhi is one of the isolated and mountainous counties of Idaho. It is pre-eminently a mining county, though it has other splendid resources. As early as the summer of 1866, a party of prospectors found their way into this mountain region and discovered rich placer diggings seventeen miles west of the present town of Salmon City, at a place called Leesburg or Salmon River Basin, and an influx of miners was the result. The basin was in Idaho County, the county seat of which was at Florence, 600 miles distant by the nearest traveled route. By an act of the territorial legislature in 1869, Idaho County was divided and the county of Lemhi created and organized. Placer mining is still being carried on extensively in several districts of the county, the area of placer mining ground yet unworked being very large. The large number of mining districts within the county precludes the possibility of particular mention, but the facts that Lemhi has held so large a percentage of her mining population, and that a large amount of capital has been attracted to the county and permanently invested in mining enterprises, afford sufficient proofs that this industry is on a permanent and sure footing.

Salmon City is the county seat of Lemhi County. It is pleasantly situated at the junction of Lemhi and Salmon rivers. It was laid out in 1867, and is surrounded by a rich agricultural region. The supplies for Leesburg and several other mining camps are transported upon pack animals, but the camps down the river are supplied by flatboats which are built at Salmon City. These boats never return to the scene where they were built, owing to the rapid current. After reaching their destination and discharging their cargo, the boats are taken to pieces and the nails and lumber used for other purposes.

As an agricultural region, the valleys of the Lemhi, Salmon and Pahsamari cannot be surpassed. Wheat, oats, barley and all kinds of vegetables return as large a yield per acre as in the great Snake River Valley. The county's share of patented and improved lands is some 20,000 acres. The immense undeveloped resources of Lemhi offer a standing protest against the long and unaccountable delay in the matter of providing railroad transportation. Though the surface of the county is mountainous, it offers no greater engineering difficulties than are found in numerous other sections through which railroads have been constructed. Recent surveys, very carefully made, through the heart of this mountainous region, with a view of building a road from Butte, Mont., to Boise City, in Idaho, fully proved that a railroad is easily practicable at a moderate cost per mile. With this road or any other built, every branch of industry and the development of every interest of the county would receive a new impetus, and thus a rich and interesting mountain community would move at once into its proper place in the very first rank among the wealthiest counties of the state. Lemhi County is also deserving of special notice as being the home of one of Idaho's United States senators, George L. Shoup. It was here that he made his first home many years ago, when Idaho was a young territory and when the county in which he settled was an isolated and sparsely inhabited portion of the Western wilderness. When public duties permit, it is to his old home in Lemhi County, where he still has his residence and where he conducts a large business, that Senator Shoup loves to return and enjoy what falls to his share, in a very busy life, of comfort and leisure.

NEZ PERCE COUNTY.

The one that could be called an historical county is that of Nez Perce, which has borne that name from the earliest days of Idaho Territory and when she was at least six times as large as the present area. It embraced what is now Idaho, Latah and Shoshone counties. A glance at the map will portray the immense area covered by old Nez Perce. Even now the country included within her limits covers nearly the entire Nez Perce Indian Reservation, which alone sums up about 275,000 acres of the very best agricultural, timber and grazing lands. The majority of the farmers of the county give their attention greatly to diversified farming, but one would hardly suppose this to be when it is stated that about 1,000,000 bushels of grain is harvested each year. The yield in all cereals here is up to the average for this country. It must be remembered that Nez Perce embraces a part of the Palouse and Potlatch agricultural districts, and these are acknowledged the leading grain-producing sections of the entire Northwest. The low altitude which so greatly favors the country along the Snake and Clearwater rivers in the county of Nez Perce has caused it to be the banner fruit-raising section of the state. In the vicinity of Lewiston the fruit yield exceeds even that of the semi-tropical valleys of California. It will be noticed that the altitude is but 650 feet above sea level, and the climate makes the entire year nothing more than a mild and refreshing spring or summer day. Now, for comparison, we will quote Mr. J. H. Evans, manager of the Riverside Fruit Farm near Lewiston. Among other things, Mr. Evans in his monograph on grape culture says:

"In calling attention of horticulturists to the Snake River Valley as a grape-producing region, it will be with reference to the growth of the foreign varieties, not that the natives may be grown here with even more ease, but where the foreign can be successfully produced the natives become of insignificant importance. The grape has proved itself adapted to so great a diversity of soils that if the climatic conditions are suitable it may be safely concluded that any good orchard land will be found adapted for the vineyard. This being true, the object of this article will be to show the favorable climatic conditions here existing. To those unacquainted with the meteorological conditions of the Pacific Coast, and especially this far inland north region, it may appear strange that here should be found an almost summer tropical climate. This surprise will be greater to those who have been inclined to regard the degrees of heat and cold simply as so many degrees of latitude from the equator without taking into account the modifying influences that may intervene to ameliorate the extremes of heat or cold that would otherwise exist. Riverside, on Snake River, is in latitude 46 degrees 25 minutes. Places on this parallel in the Atlantic States would have long, severe, cold winters, a short summer and a humid atmosphere. Here the conditions are almost reversed. The winters are mild and short, the summers long, hot and dry. Did space permit, it would be interesting to review the conditions that conspire to produce the climatic effects, but that they exist will be shown further on. The culture of the grape has received more scientific study and research than any other fruit; through years of continued observation French savants have demonstrated the number of degrees, daily mean temperature, necessary to cause the vines to leaf out, also the number of degrees of heat necessary to produce the bloom and ripe fruit. It is stated for the period of a month following the appearance of the seeds, the mean temperature should not fall below 66.2 degrees Fahrenheit, and that 63 degrees is the lowest at which grapes will ripen, and that the mean heat of the period from the vegetation of the vine to the ripening of the fruit must be at least 59 degrees. That the most important season is twenty days prior to the ripening of the fruit, during which time the mean daily temperature should be 73.5 degrees. Now, to prove that the Snake River Valley receives sufficient heat to perfectly ripen the grape, as shown by the French tests given above, attention is called to the following table, compiled from the report of the chief signal officer of the United States Army for the year 1889. Lewiston, Idaho, situated at the confluence of the Clearwater and Snake rivers, is only three miles from Riverside, the point on Snake River to which particular attention is called. For the sake of comparison, several well-known centres of fruit growing in California are included in the list. From the table it will also be seen that the Snake River not only possesses the requisite degree of heat for the proper development of the grape in its various stages of growth as required in the authorities quoted above, but in this respect compares favorably with the most noted grape-growing sections of California. It may be suggested by some that the high temperature and dry atmosphere which here prevail, while highly conducive to grape growing, might be detrimental to other fruits. Space will only permit a brief reply, and that is, that when the deficient rainfall has been supplemented by irrigation the horticulturist who desires to make a specialty of either berries, apples, peaches, nectarines, apricots, prunes, plums, cherries, or pears can engage in the enterprise with the full assurance of success. The Snake River Valley has already achieved a wide reputation for the fine quality of the peaches, and the pears will compare favorably with those produced in the finest fruit-growing regions of the world."

	April.	May.	June.	July.	August	Sept.	Mean.
Lewiston, Idaho...	60°	66°	73.5°	81.5°	75°	60.1°	69.3°
San Jose, Cal......	59.7°	61.9°	66.2°	66.1°	66.2°	69.7°	64.6°
Sacramento, Cal...	58.6°	61.4°	67.8°	68.3°	67.1°	63.4°	64.4°
Fresno, Cal........	63.5°	69.6°	79.5°	82.6°	83.2°	73.6°	75.5°
Santa Clara, Cal...	59.8°	61.9°	66.3°	64.6°	66.3°	66.9°	64.3°
Vacaville, Cal......	61°	64.9°	72.5°	74.4°	75.5°	74.5°	71.3°
Los Angeles, Cal...	62.2°	62.6°	66.4°	70.8°	71.6°	72.6°	67.7°
San Diego, Cal......	61.8°	63.2°	64.9°	69°	73°	70.8°	66.9°

Lewiston.

From the summit of the hill, on the Uniontown stage line, the Lewiston country lies to the southward like a panorama, between 2,000 and 3,000 feet below. The Clearwater River crosses the foreground like a ribbon of silver, and on the right unites with the Snake, whose yellow tide immediately suggests the precious metal which has been washed from its treasure-laden bars by the millions of dollars, and the oddly contrasted streams, thus wedded, carry the products of hundreds of generous orchards on to the mighty Columbia. The deep green fringe of fruit farms and ornamental trees which line the opposite bank of the Clearwater widens at the confluence of the two streams into a richly wooded park, whose avenues are dotted with the splendid homes of the town of Lewiston, Idaho. Behind this rises a bluff from 50 to 100 feet, from which recedes a gently rolling plain for some 30 miles to the foot of Craig's Mountain on the left and 60 miles to the Blue Mountains on the right. Each of these ranges runs nearly to the centre of the picture, where they break off abruptly, leaving a gateway through which the Snake River flows to the northward. On either side of the streets in Lewiston are rows of tall poplars, with here and there a catalpa or a spreading honey locust to break the monotony of the line. The dooryards are decorated with a profusion of beautiful flowers, only to be seen in the irrigated districts. Among these pretty modern homes may still be found a few grand old monuments of pioneer days in the shape of great log houses with their long porches and moss-grown clapboard roofs. A few of these are still occupied and have neatly whitewashed split picket fences. Over the entire town is a network of irrigating ditches, varying from the size of small rivers to the tiniest streamlets. Along the larger ones are picturesque old moss-grown water-wheels. These are similar to the side wheel of a steamer and are turned by the current of the stream or canal in which they are hung. Around the edges they have cans or buckets which carry the water up as the wheel revolves and discharge their burdens at the top in a trough or flume, with a rhythmic splash, keeping time to the squeaking of the axle, making a veritable orchestra. On every side is beauty, comfort and cheerfulness. Lewiston seems to be exempt from all common curses. Irrigated orchards cannot suffer from drought. With the ten months of summer there are no frosts to fear. The superiority of the fruit always assures it a ready market in spite of the general supply and demand. And besides all this is the blessing of a glorious climate.

Lewiston was settled shortly after Walla Walla, for the date of settlement runs back to 1861. The gold excitement at that time in Shoshone and Idaho counties was the impetus which promoted Lewiston to a city of several thousand. The town was named for or in honor of Captain Meriwether Lewis, of the famous Lewis-Clarke exploring party sent out by President Thomas Jefferson in 1803 to 1805. Ever since Lewiston has been a town it has not confined its enormous trade to the retail business. It has acted a prominent part in wholesaling goods to all points on or tributary to the Clearwater and Snake rivers. That which has been the prime factor in keeping Lewiston from growing to a city of great importance has been the lack of railroad transportation. However, it is a just pleasure to its inhabitants to know that the transcontinental lines, reaching for every branch of this prolific region, must acknowledge the importance of this point as a shipping centre, and treat it as such. Just as soon as Lewiston has trains running into the city, population will grow to an enormous extent, and the property embraced in the limits of the Garden City will be held at a high figure. The river transportation facilities are inadequate for the shipment of the products of the Lewiston fruit and grain belt. Visitors to Lewiston now wonder at the products of the country, but they are greatly surprised to know that the tributary fruit lands are not worked to the limit, owing to the want of railroads to carry out their products. Both the Northern and Union Pacific Railroad systems have lines surveyed into Lewiston, and there is no doubt that within a short time the Great Northern will be reaching for this section. From surveys already made it is more than probable that Lewiston will, in the near future, be on the main line of a transcontinental railroad. Lewiston, similar to Walla Walla, has many wealthy residents, who are thoroughly devoted to their beautiful town. Substantial business blocks are to be found here. Lewiston may proudly boast of the handsomest bank building in the State of Idaho, which is built out of native stone, found in the immediate neighborhood. The town is amply supplied with schools and churches of all denominations. It being the county seat of Nez Perce County, a commodious courthouse affords accommodations for the duties of her officials.

It is of importance to add that less wind prevails at this point than any other place reported by the Signal Service.

The timbered lands of Nez Perce County are estimated at 200,000 acres, all of which is covered with the very finest lumber material. Grazing lands may be found in a most prolific state, and stock raising is carried on extensively while at the same time it is not considered a chief industry.

The general government of Nez Perce County is carried out in a dignified degree, and the county in general may be classed as a typical Eastern section. Society is of a cultured state and her people sustain the dignity of their position.

OWYHEE COUNTY.

Following the discoveries of gold on the tributaries of the Boise River in 1862, an era of persistent and extensive prospecting set in, and a wild spirit of adventurous gold-seeking pushed the restless crowds of treasure hunters in all directions throughout the mountain sections of Southern Idaho.

The prospectors of 1863 were in search of placer gold, and while making their way into the fastnesses of the Owyhee Mountains found some light deposits of the precious metal on a stream which they called Jordan's Creek, from the name of one of their number. Little satisfied with this result, they pushed their operations farther into the mountains, where, after much fruitless labor, privations, hardships and dangers, they were rewarded by the discovery of rich croppings, which led to the uncovering of some of the richest gold and silver mines ever found on the continent, and to the opening and settlement of a large, important and interesting section of Idaho, which has long had its place on the map as Owyhee County. This county covers a large area, and has a diversified surface of mountain plains and valleys. It extends from the Snake River on the north to the Nevada line on the south, and from the Oregon line on the west to the line on the east which separates it from the county of Cassia. With an area of not less than 6,500 square miles, the county has a population of about 4,000, the greater portion of which is employed in mining, though the agricultural and stock-raising interests are very considerable. The mining districts cover a large mountain area, containing many very rich mines, the yield from some of which in the past have been almost fabulous, though in none of these mines have the explorations been to any considerable depth compared to that attained in other mining regions. Recent developments show that these Owyhee mines have lost nothing of their first value or of their promise of future productiveness. An interesting episode in the history of Owyhee County, and one which cannot in justice be omitted, is that in relation to the discovery within her borders of diamonds, opals, rubies, moss agates and other precious stones.

Diamonds have not yet been found in any alarming quantities, but the persistent prospecting resulted in the discovery of rare and beautiful opals of nearly every size and character, the magnificent and flashing fire opal predominating. These opal beds have been found in several localities in Owyhee County, and scarcely a week passes that new and surprising discoveries are not made. The discovery is a very important one, and it has already given rise to a new industry which well deserves the praise it has won among the resources of Owyhee County.

The present annual output of all the gold and silver mines of Owyhee County is estimated at $1,500,000, which could be indefinitely increased by a wise and liberal expenditure of capital. In some of the older districts recent developments have brought to light millions of dollars worth of good ore where very much lighter results were expected. This is particularly true with regard to some of the older mines near Silver City, embracing those on the flanks of War Eagle Mountain. In one of the new districts, that in which the great De Lamar Mine is situated, the discoveries and results make it probable that the district is destined to equal in richness of ores and value of output those of he great Comstock in Nevada. Of the De Lamar Mine, Gov. George L. Shoup, now United States Senator from Idaho, in his report to the Secretary of the Interior in the year 1890 wrote as follows: "The latest information from the mines at De Lamar are of the most encouraging character. Development work has gone on systematically and the ore now in sight is estimated at from $3,000,000 to $4,000,000. Mills with improvements of the latest and best inventions have been erected. It is said that $2,000,000 have been offered for the De Lamar mining system and declined. The greatest need of the place now is railway communication to take ore out and bring in timber and mining supplies. The present output of the mines is said to average $60,000 per month."

Since the publication of this report something less than a controlling interest in the property has been sold to an English syndicate, and the work of development and improvement has been pushed on a large scale, but during the same time the output has been increased to between $80,000 and $100,000 per month, more than half of which has been net profit, and a much larger percentage would have been saved in profit but for the lack of railway communication. Each succeeding month's work reveals more extensive and richer ore bodies and makes necessary additional improvements and facilities for extracting and crushing the ores. When it is considered that much of this ore, which is of such a nature that it must be taken to distant reduction works for treatment, and must be hauled by teams from 30 to 60 miles to the nearest point on the Oregon Short Line, the imperative necessity of railway communication is at once apparent. From what has already been done, and from the present character and outlook of the mines, an annual output in the early future of $5,000,000 is not an extravagant estimate or prediction.

Great as is the mineral wealth of the county, its agricultural and stock-raising interests form a very important part of its resources. In 1890 Governor Shoup reported of improved and patented lands within the county 15,028 acres, at an assessed valuation of nearly $309,000, and of improved lands unpatented, 40,000 acres, valuation $87,000. These settled and cultivated lands are very fertile and productive, and are distributed among several large and beautiful valleys, the principal of which are the Bruneau and the Upper Owyhee valleys. All these valleys are well watered, have a mild and salubrious climate and all the other natural advantages to make them what they are, the pleasant home spots of an industrious and thrifty people. Since 1890 the growth in population and the march of improvement have been rapid, but in the absence of reliable data this increase cannot be accurately noted. Enough has been said, however, to show that the agricultural resources of the county are all that could be expected or desired. Of stock raising, the Governor reported 16,000 head of stock cattle, 15,000 range horses and 75,000 sheep. Since this report was made the progress and increase of this resource have kept pace with the advance made in other interests and industries. The grazing lands are almost limitless in extent, the melting snows of the Owyhee range nourishing a most prolific growth of native grasses. A very important feature of the stock-raising industry is found in the natural division of the pastoral lands into winter and summer ranges. On the comparatively level lands adjacent to the Snake River and its tributaries the peculiar species of sagebrush grows, which is known as the white sage. The white sage lands cover a vast area where the snowfall is inconsiderable and the winters are always mild. During winter the stock feed upon this white sage and keep fat, and are thus ready to move with advancing spring toward the foothills and mountains, feeding upon the tender young grass as it follows the melting snows on the flanks of the mountains. Thus large herds of stock have been kept upon this unrivaled natural pasture for a long series of years, while the pasturage itself has continued to improve, and to-day shows a capability of sustaining more than four times the amount of stock that is now being kept upon it.

For extent of area, diversified surface, fine climate, varied and rich resources and all the conditions conducing to health and prosperity, Owyhee County certainly deserves to occupy a place in the very foremost rank among the many prosperous communities of Idaho.

ONEIDA COUNTY.

The resources of this county are chiefly those of agriculture and stock raising. There are about 60,000 acres of patented and improved lands and nearly 50,000 acres of unpatented lands, but which are claimed and occupied, and which are, to a large extent, improved and cultured. Immense herds of horses, cattle and sheep find excellent pasturage the year round upon the splendid stock range, the capabilities of which for stock raising have as yet scarcely begun to be taxed. The central portion of Oneida County contains the county capital, beautifully situated in a broad and fertile valley and surrounded by a fine farming and stock-raising country. Malad City is a handsome town, has excellent hotels, schools and private residences, a local newspaper, and holds a very large retail trade. The southeastern portion of the county is traversed by the Union Pacific Railway, which connects the railroad system of Utah with the Northern Pacific in Montana. This road was originally narrow gauge, but the constantly swelling volume of business several years ago compelled a change to standard gauge. The traffic on the road is now enormous and constantly increasing. The western portion of the county is more mountainous and less developed every way. The northern portion is traversed by the Union Pacific system, which connects the old line at Granger with the Oregon system. This branch of the system forms a very important link in one of the principal transcontinental lines of railway, and has been, since its completion, the favorite route of tourists and general traffic. The whole of the northwestern portion of this county is admirably adapted to stock raising, and also embraces several well-watered valleys, capable of supporting a prosperous community of farmers. Magnificent forests of pine timber exist in the central and western sections of the county. The home supply of fuel and lumber in sight is ample for many generations to come. In the Malad Valley good indications of coal have been found.

This county is a noble illustration of what industry, economy and perseverance under difficulties will do. The first settlers found the country an apparently hopeless and sterile desert; but faith and courage and tireless industry have changed the face of the erstwhile barren wilderness and converted the desert like scenes into fertile farms, and prosperous and happy homes. Much yet remains to be done, but the same strong and noble qualities are inherent in the people, and the same forces will conquer the remaining area to peace, prosperity and civilization.

SHOSHONE COUNTY.

The first advent of white occupants into the extensive mountain region embraced within the present boundaries of Shoshone County occurred in the summer of 1860, when a small party of adventurous prospectors discovered rich deposits of placer gold on a small tributary of Oro Fino Creek, a stream which flows into the South Clearwater, a few miles from its junction with the northern branch. These were the first discoveries of the precious metals made within what is now the State of Idaho. At that time the entire vast mountain region drained by the waters of the Salmon and Clearwater rivers formed a part of the Territory of Washington. During the spring and summer of 1861 placer gold was found in paying quantities on nearly all the tributaries of the Clearwater. The excitement caused by this discovery was in-

IDAHO—THE GEM OF THE MOUNTAINS.

tense and widespread, and attracted thousands of miners and representatives of all classes, who are usually awakened into activity by a new gold excitement. The peopling of these mountains by thousands of eager gold-seekers was soon followed by the building of towns, that of Lewiston being the first, and by acts of the Washington Territorial Legislature creating and organizing the counties of Nez Perce and Shoshone. During the ten years following the discovery the placer mines of the northern portion of Shoshone County yielded up many millions of dollars of yellow gold dust. Then began the period of exhaustion, which soon left but a handful of white miners in the county, the bulk of the mining population being Chinese, who continued to hold on tenaciously and worked the ground which the white miners had found unremunerative. Matters looked blue for old Shoshone County, but her small white population stayed with her, managed to keep in running order an excellent county government, and learned to supplement their resources with those of farming and stock raising on a small scale. The western portion of the county has quite a large area of good grazing land, lying perched on a broad tableland, which affords the finest summer range for stock, and partly on the sheltered slopes of the hills bordering the Clearwater, where stock can be kept in good condition during the severest winters, with but little care or extra feeding. The forests also afford an inexhaustible supply of the finest timber adapted to the growing demand for lumber, millions of feet of which are annually cut and rafted down the Clearwater to Lewiston and to points below. With all this, however, the historical county would have had a hard row to hoe but for the touch of the Aladdin lamp which gladdened the eyes of the miner when the great treasure house of the Cœur d'Alene region was opened to his view. This presented him with a new field for his favorite pursuits, wherein there were unbounded possibilities which filled his heart with renewed courage and hope.

Westward from the summit of the Bitter Root Mountains to the eastern boundary of Kootenai County and from the southern drainage slope of the St. Joe Valley to the Cœur d'Alene Mountains on the north, comprises the present great mining region of Shoshone County. This wide region of mountain and gulch, covered with a dense growth of pine, fir, tamarack and cedar and drained by the St. Joe and Cœur d'Alene rivers and their tributaries, was comparatively unknown until 1884, when the discovery of placer gold by Prichard and his associates in the creek now bearing his name excited the stampede which quickly populated the valleys of the North and South forks of the Cœur d'Alene River with from 4,000 to 5,000 hardy men. The search for extensive rich and easily worked placers was not so successful as it had been in the old Oro Fino district of the same county, or in other sections of Idaho where placer gold deposits were first found, but the results were upon the whole satisfactory, and for many years the aggregate output of placer gold was enormous. The area of virgin placer ground in this section of the Cœur d'Alene region is yet very large, and it will continue to be profitably worked for an indefinite time to come. The discovery of galena, or what is known as lead-silver ores, was made in the same year on a tributary of the South Fork of the Cœur d'Alene. This was soon followed by the discovery of the famous Bunker Hill and Sullivan mines on a neighboring tributary of the same stream. This last find was of such extraordinary magnitude and richness as to awaken the interests of Montana capitalists in the country, and in the ensuing years they commenced the construction of concentrating works and the building of a narrow-gauge railroad to connect the mines with a station on the Northern Pacific Railroad. This was the wedge which opened the marvelous treasures of the Cœur d'Alene to the world and which enabled it within less than three years to become what has since been the greatest lead-producing region in the United States. Since then both the Northern Pacific and Union Pacific companies have extended their lines into this mining region, which not only affords ample transportation facilities for the mines already discovered and worked, but which will also stimulate discovery in a region much of which yet remains unprospected and encourage the full development of the thousands of valuable mineral prospects now lying dormant. Since mining begun in this section of the county many new and flourishing towns have sprung up in the respective neighborhoods of the principal groups of mines. Murray, the county seat, is situated on Prichard Creek, in the centre of the gold belt. The town is very handsomely situated, has a population of about 1,200, and is the centre of a healthy trade. In the lead and silver producing districts on the South Fork of the Cœur d'Alene and its tributaries are found the towns of Wardner, Mullan, Wallace, Burke, Osborne, Gem and several others. The real wealth of the county is chiefly in its lead-silver mines and in the large population of industrious miners and workers of every class which these mines have attracted and will continue to attract and hold. The gold-mining industry will also continue to add an important item to the aggregate wealth. The drawbacks that are felt at present are the reduced price of lead and silver and the effects, yet felt, of recent labor troubles. But these adverse conditions and circumstances must, in the nature of things, prove only temporary and transitory. There is too much mineral wealth buried in these mountains, and it is too badly needed in the current of trade, to permit of long delay in making it available for the use of the world. The magnificent forests of Shoshone County cover an immense area, with a practically inexhaustible supply of material for all the purposes for which this timber is needed. Increasing settlement and new lines of transportation will carry portions of these forests for us annually, but by far the greater will remain as a reserve source of wealth for future generations.

WASHINGTON COUNTY.

Not every county in the state can present to the readers of Idaho's souvenir so many varied resources as does the rich and prolific county of Washington, which lies in the southwestern portion of the state, covering an area of about 3,750 square miles. The resources consist chiefly, however, of agriculture, stock, timber and mining. The income from either of these industries has proved a great factor in the building up of a most attractive and wealthy district. The agricultural district extends along Weiser River, where diversified products are grown to a high degree of perfection. The altitude of Weiser Valley is 2,000 feet above sea level, which adapts that section to fruit growing in all its branches. The climate may be judged when it is stated that corn grows as readily in Weiser Valley as in Illinois or Iowa. The valleys in the northern part of the county yield immense amounts of wheat, barley, oats and hay, the average production of wheat being 40 bushels per acre. Weiser Valley proper, in which is situated the beautiful little city of Weiser, extends along both sides of Weiser River for a distance of 25 miles, with an average width of 5 miles. At a cost of $45,000, an irrigating canal 20 miles in length has been constructed on the west side of Weiser River, which supplies water for 35,000 acres of this matchless field. This body of land is nearly all settled with an energetic and progressive class of people, who have in course of cultivation teeming orchards of prunes, apples, etc., and all kinds of vegetables and cereals. The products of this district are shipped to a very considerable extent to Eastern Idaho and Montana points. This county is noted for its stock-feeding qualities, owing to the immense crops of clover and alfalfa hay that are harvested.

The many valleys that are equally productive in Washington County cannot receive the amount of space that we should like to devote to them, but they may all be classed among the first rank of the better fruit and grain producing districts in the Northwest. Among these valleys are Mann's Creek, Middle, Salubria, Crane Creek, Indian, Council and Horses valleys and Salmon meadows. Each of these valleys have an unprecedented reputation for grain growing and stock raising, and they are always encouraged by the good market that awaits the disposal of their crops and herds. It is important to note that there is in the upper valleys of Weiser a large quantity of lands that need no irrigation to produce crops. Innumerable creeks not exhibited upon the map are tributaries to the Weiser River and supply large bodies of farms with the necessary irrigation for farm purposes. The grazing lands of Washington County are very extensive, and abound in natural grasses, upon which about 30,000 cattle, 25,000 horses and 125,000 sheep find an abundance of wholesome food. The timber embraced in this county will be a surprise to many who have been long acquainted with the other resources of Washington, but have never looked into her wonderful forests of unrivaled timber. The area covered by this important item is 900 square miles. The quality and quantity to be found in Washington County is not even excelled in the forest districts of the states of Washington and Oregon, and the Weiser River, which passes directly through the timber belt, affords a cheap means of transportation to the railroad at Weiser City.

While Washington County can present statistics on grain, fruits and timber that will be met with envy by many older and richer sections, she presents with great pride, her mining industries as being second to but very few counties in the state. About 25 miles from Weiser is the mining camp of Mineral, which is the centre of a group of silver mines which are rapidly becoming noted and productive. The ores are of the smelting and concentrating classes, and are to be found in large bodies. The principal mines in this district are the Maria, Blackhawk, Boone, Silver Belle, Atlanta, Egan, Muldoon and Little Chief. The maximum width of the veins is over 60 feet in the Boone, 10 in the Maria and 15 in the Blackhawk. The average assay value of the smelting ore is 50 ounces of silver; of the concentrating ore, 15 ounces. The facilities for the reduction of ores are beyond those to be found anywhere in the Northwest. The porphyrite smelter, erected in 1889, and the mutual smelter, recently completed and now in full operation, each have a capacity of 30 tons daily. The output for 1890, derived wholly from the porphyrite smelter, was nearly $70,000. The total number of mines and claims now working are over 50. The output for 1891 was $190,000, and it was estimated that the Blackhawk Company would make the output in 1892 reach $300,000. That which has attracted the most attention in mining circles in Washington County for some time is the district known as the Seven Devils. This is the great copper region of Idaho, and promises to rival the famous mines of Montana. One mine here has the largest surface showing of any mine in the world; the surface outcrop is over 75,000 tons of copper, which assays 20 per cent. This promises to be one of the largest camps in the West, if not in the world. The ores carry considerable gold and silver, besides the copper. A projected railroad from Weiser touches this mining district. Coal has been found within ten miles of Weiser. Great developments are expected, as the veins are extensive and of good quality. Several large bodies of mica have been found and some of the groups bonded.

The city of Weiser, the county seat of Washington County and the natural centre and only outlet for the immense country tributary to it, is beautifully located on the north bank of the Weiser River, on the Union Pacific Railway, and has an imposing site for a town. While the town is young, it ranks very high as a business point and is the commercial centre for a vast portion of country outside of the county in which it is situated. An immense mill is in operation at this place, and it is the supply point for a large majority of the larger towns in this section of the state. Weiser is well situated for a railway centre, and it is claimed that the only practical route for the Union Pacific to connect with Northern Idaho is up the Weiser River from this point. The amount of business for the city of Weiser was estimated last year as follows: Silver, $550,000; gold, $100,000; copper, $200,000; wool, 650,000 pounds, $90,000; cattle, 80 carloads shipped in May, $40,000; sheep, shipped in May, $50,000; horses, 15 carloads shipped in May, $12,000; barley, 250,000 bushels, $150,000; wheat, 600,000 bushels, $100,000; oats, 250,000 bushels, $150,000; hay, 10,000 tons, $75,000; Total, $1,517,000. Fruits, vegetables and other products figure largely in the output, which have not been estimated in the foregoing figures.

ORCHARD AT BLUE LAKES.

SHOSHONE FALLS.

STREET IN LEWISTON

A PIONEER SCHOOL, TAUGHT BY MRS. ELLA BEHJSNER.

MOUTH OF ST. JOE.

CHIEF GERRY OF THE SPOKANES.

BUILDINGS AND GROUNDS OF THE PAYETTE NURSERIES.
Payette, Canyon County, W. G. Winhery, Proprietor

GRANGEVILLE, IDAHO.

COTTONWOOD, IDAHO.

REPRESENTATIVE CITIZENS.

Idaho is justly proud of the men who have added so much to the upbuilding of the state. In this number will be found a page devoted to the legislature, state and federal officers, and men who, by their untiring efforts, have brought credit not only upon themselves but upon the state. It may be noticed that there are missing biographies of a few of the legislators as well as the portrait of Hon. Willis H. Sweet, representative in Congress. The publisher was unsuccessful in his attempt to procure them, and they are therefore unavoidably omitted.

HON. WM. J. MCCONNELL, the present Governor of Idaho, was born in Commerce, Oakland County, Michigan, on Sept. 18, 1839. His early life was spent upon the farm, receiving his education in the common schools and academies of his state, alternately teaching and attending school after he was sixteen up to the time he was twenty years of age. In the spring of 1860 he started overland to California. Being without money upon reaching the Missouri River, he hired out to drive a six-mule team to Salt Lake City and successfully accomplished the feat, although he had never had his hands on a mule before. Fifty-three days were consumed in the trip, for which he received $1 per day. Arriving in California he engaged in mining during the winters of 1860-61 and 1861-62 with indifferent success. He went to Portland, and meeting some farmers from the Willamette Valley who were inquiring for a school-teacher, he went with them into the country and engaged in teaching school during the remainder of the summer and following winter. He was appointed Deputy United States Marshal under Alvord, and had charge of the head office in Boise City in 1865-66. In the fall of '66 Mr. McConnell returned to Oregon, where he had been engaged in teaching before coming to Idaho, and married a young lady there and returned to Humboldt County, California, engaging in the cattle business for five years, after which he again returned to Oregon and interested himself in merchandising and in politics, soon after opening a large mercantile establishment in the northern part of Idaho, but still continuing his residence in Oregon, until 1887, when he moved his family to his present home in Moscow, Idaho. He took a prominent part in the convention which framed the present constitution of the State of Idaho; went to Washington and assisted in securing the admission of the state, and was elected one of the first senators that represented Idaho in the United States Senate. He was there during the short term of the Fifty-first Congress, having secured the shortest term in drawing for place; but while there he was noted for his activity and the promptness with which he entered into the questions of the day. When only a few days in the Senate, he made a speech on the silver question, and on the sixteenth of February, 1891, he made his memorable speech on the bonded indebtedness of the Union Pacific Railroad. Mr. McConnell is a type of the self-made American. What he has accomplished he owes to his own energy and determination to succeed. He has ever proven himself a foeman worthy of any champion's steel, whether in debate or otherwise. His term of office as Governor of Idaho expires Jan. 1, 1895.

GEORGE L. SHOUP, United States Senator from Idaho, was born in Kittanning, Armstrong County, Pennsylvania, June 15, 1836. He was educated in the public schools of Freeport and Slate Lick. In June, 1852, moved with his father to Illinois, and was engaged in farming and stock raising near Galesburg until 1858. In 1859 he removed to Colorado, where he was engaged in the mining and mercantile business until 1861. In September, 1861, enlisted in a company of scouts and was soon thereafter commissioned Second Lieutenant. During the autumn and winter of 1861 he was engaged in scouting along the base of the Rocky Mountains. Was ordered to New Mexico in 1862, and was kept on scouting duty until 1863, and while in that territory was promoted to First Lieutenant. He was then ordered to the Arkansas River. In May, 1863, he was assigned to the First Colorado Regiment of Cavalry. In 1864 he was elected to the Constitutional Convention to prepare a constitution for the proposed State of Colorado, and obtained leave of absence for thirty days to serve as a member of said convention. After performing this service he returned to active duty in the army, was commissioned Colonel of the Third Colorado Cavalry in September, 1864, and was mustered out in Denver with the regiment at the expiration of his term of service. He engaged in the mercantile business in Virginia City, Mont., in 1866, and during the same year established a business at Salmon City, Idaho. Since 1866 he has been engaged in the mining, stock-raising, mercantile and other business in Idaho. He was a member of the Eighth and Tenth Territorial Legislatures. Was a delegate to the National Republican Convention in 1880. Was a member of the Republican National Committee from 1880 until 1884. Was United States Commissioner for Idaho at the World's Cotton Centennial Exposition at New Orleans, La., in 1884-85, and was again placed on the Republican National Committee in 1888. He was appointed Governor of Idaho Territory in March, 1889, which position he held until elected Governor of the State of Idaho, Oct. 1, 1890, and was elected to the United States Senate, as a Republican, Dec. 18, 1890, and took his seat December 29th of the same year. His term of service will expire March 3, 1895.

LIEUTENANT GOVERNOR WILLIS was born at Parishville, St. Lawrence County, New York, Oct. 20, 1844. He was educated at the State Normal School at Potsdam, N. Y., and attended the Poughkeepsie Business College. At the age of twenty he engaged in the mercantile business at Red Wing, Minn. Two years later he went to Deer Lodge, Mont., and engaged in mining. In the fall of 1866 he moved to Bannock, Mont., and two years later moved to Lemhi County, Idaho, where he was engaged in mining until the winter of 1879, when he moved to Challis, his present home, and engaged in the livery business. For ten years he was Assessor of Custer County, and in the fall of 1891 was made Grand Master of the Odd Fellows of Idaho. Lieutenant Governor Willis was elected to his honored position at the November election, and has conducted the affairs of his office in an able and efficient manner. He is a great favorite among the people.

GEN. JAMES F. CURTIS, Secretary of State for Idaho, was born in the State of Massachusetts, and has been a resident of the Pacific Coast States since 1848. General Curtis has a noted military record, having served in the volunteers as Colonel of the Fourth Regiment of Cavalry during the War of the Rebellion. During his residence in Idaho, General Curtis has acted a prominent role in the politics of the state, and was Adjutant General of the State, which gave him command of the Idaho militia during the recent mining labor troubles in the Cœur d' Alene district in 1892. At the November election, General Curtis was elected, by an overwhelming majority, to the office which he so handsomely fills.

HON. GEO. M. PARSONS was born, in Cambridge City, Ind., Jan. 15, 1850, and was educated in the public schools of Cincinnati and Hamilton, Ohio. He was a soldier at fifteen years of age, enlisting and serving as a private soldier during the last year of the Civil War, in Company F, One Hundred and Eighty-Ninth Ohio Volunteer Infantry. He came to Idaho in 1871, and has resided here ever since. He was a member of the Seventh and Tenth Idaho Legislatures. Was Probate Judge of Alturas County, Idaho, during 1883 and 1884. He was admitted to the bar in 1885, and elected Attorney General of the State of Idaho, Nov. 8, 1892.

HON. FRANK C. RAMSEY was born in Fulton County, Pennsylvania, in the year 1855. He was educated in the common schools and the Iron City Business College. Owing to poor health, he moved to the State of Ohio in 1872, where he resided three years and then moved to Iowa. After spending several years there on a farm, he removed to Kansas and from there to Colorado, where he was engaged in stock raising. In 1884 he decided to locate and moved to Idaho, where he devoted his time to the business of stock raising. He was elected to the legislature three years ago and complimented with the office of State Auditor at the last election. He was at one time Assessor of Cassia County, and later published and edited a newspaper at Pocatello. Mr. Ramsey enjoys the confidence of the entire state and makes an efficient and conscientious official.

HON. WILLIAM C. HILL, State Treasurer for Idaho, was born in the city of St. Louis, Mo., in the year 1846, where he attended college until eighteen years of age. He was engaged in the wholesale mercantile business in that city from 1864 until 1870. In the spring of 1871 he moved to Denver, Co., where he was engaged in the mercantile business until the spring of 1883, when he removed to Idaho, of which state he has ever since been a resident. Mr. Hill was elected State Treasurer Nov. 8, 1892. He has the interests of the state at heart and makes an efficient officer.

PROF. B. BYRON LOWER, State Superintendent of Public Instruction, was born at Liberty Mills, Ind., May 7, 1861. In 1865 he moved to Isabella County, Michigan, where he was reared on a farm and attended the customary district school during the winter. He afterward attended the Mount Pleasant School, where he graduated in 1881. After three years of teaching he attended the Northern Indiana Normal School at Valparaiso for two years, at the end of which time he graduated. He removed to Idaho in the fall of 1887, where he has been engaged in educational circles and was recently elected to his present position. Superintendent Lower is very devoted to his duties and will undoubtedly prove a credit to himself as well as to his state.

HON. JOS. PERRAULT is a native of Montreal, Can. He came to the coast in 1864, and soon found his way to the historic old town of Lewiston in Northern Idaho. In 1872 he came to Boise and was assistant editor of the *Statesman* till 1878. In 1875 Mr. Perrault was appointed Territorial Controller and Superintendent of Public Instruction, which positions he held till 1880. In 1883 he was appointed Territorial Treasurer by Gov. Wm. M. Bunn. In 1886 he accepted the position of assistant cashier of the Boise City National Bank, the duties of which position he continued to discharge till July, 1888. He is at present a director of the bank. Mr. Perrault is also vice president of the Idaho Commercial Company, doing business at Weiser, and is a heavy stockholder in the Statesman Printing Company, and is interested in several water and irrigating enterprises for the development of the country. It goes without saying that he is and was always a Republican, active, aggressive and combative. In September, 1889, Mr. Perrault was appointed by President Harrison Receiver of the United States Land Office at Boise City.

HON. CHARLES S. KINGSLEY, Register of the United States Land Office at Boise City, Idaho, was born in Portland, Ore., in 1856. His parental ancestors were early settlers in Vermont and New York. His father, Calvin S. Kingsley, was one of the pioneers of the Pacific Northwest and was a graduate of Ann Arbor in the class of 1849. He came to Oregon by the way of the Isthmus and landed in Portland when it contained only very few inhabitants. In 1863 Calvin Kingsley went to Idaho City, in the gold fields known as the Boise Basin. From 1871 to 1877 his son Charles was kept in Michigan attending the high school at Ovid and later Olivette and Albion colleges. In 1877 he began the study of photography in the city of Baltimore. He had been a successful photographer until his appointment by President Harrison to the position he now holds. Mr. Kingsley has established his devotion to the Republican party during his many years' residence in Idaho.

IDAHO=THE GEM OF THE MOUNTAINS.

HON. JAMES H. HAWLEY was born in Dubuque, Iowa, Jan. 7, 1847. He went to California in 1861. In April, 1862, he came to Idaho, stopping first in Florence, Idaho County. From there, early in the spring of 1863, he went into Boise Basin, where he resided until 1882. From 1882 to 1886 he resided in Hailey, Alturas County, moving to Boise City in 1886, where he has since resided. From 1862 to 1877 was engaged in prospecting and mining. He was admitted as an attorney to the Supreme Court of Idaho in February, 1871. He was a member of the lower house of the Sixth Territorial Legislature, in 1870; also, Clerk of the same body in 1872. Was a member of the upper house during the eighth session in 1874; also, Clerk during the ninth session in 1876. He was a member of the Board of County Commissioners of Boise County in 1876 and 1877. During the latter year he was elected District Attorney of the Second Judicial District, comprising Boise, Alturas, Custer and Lemhi counties, and occupied that position for four years. President Cleveland appointed him United States Attorney in May, 1884, and he held the position four years. He was beaten for the nomination for delegate to Congress in the Democratic Convention by Hon. John Hailey in 1884. Was again unanimously nominated in the fall of 1888 for delegate to Congress, but was defeated by Hon. Fred T. Dubois. He was married in July, 1875, at Quartzburg, in Boise County, to Miss Mary Elizabeth Bullock. Was one of the first to turn his attention to quartz mining in Boise County, and was identified with nearly all of the early locations in the different districts in that county. Since January, 1890, has been engaged in the practice of law with William F. Reeves, Esq., with offices at Blackfoot and Boise City.

WILLIS H. PETTIT, United States Surveyor General for Idaho, was born June 6, 1835, on a farm near the town of Mishawaka, St. Joseph County, Ind. his parents (David and Elizabeth Pettit) emigrating from Miami County, Ohio, in 1832. His early education was in the common country schools and he afterward graduated at the High School in Mishawaka. On the breaking out of the War of the Rebellion, he enlisted in the first regiment leaving the state (the Ninth Infantry), served through the three-months' campaign in West Virginia and re-enlisted for the war in the Fourth Battery, Indiana Volunteer Artillery serving in all the campaigns of the Army of the Cumberland, being promoted to a lieutenancy in that battery in 1863. At the close of the war he settled in Indianapolis, Ind., engaging in business there until 1877, when he came to Idaho, and engaged in the mining business until appointed United States Surveyor General of the state by President Harrison in 1890.

HON. JOSEPH PINKHAM, United States Marshal for the State of Idaho, was born in Canada in 1832. He received a common school education and at the age of nineteen years migrated to California by the way of Cape Horn. He occupied his time in the Golden State by mining until 1853, when he moved to Oregon and spent his time in that state until 1865, when he made Idaho City, Idaho, his home. Here he was engaged in the mercantile and mining business. In 1870, President Grant appointed him United States Marshal for Idaho and reappointed him in 1874 to the same position. Upon the expiration of his term he owned and superintended a stage line through the Boise Basin. Mr. Pinkham was again appointed to the office that he held twice before, by President Harrison. He is at present acting in that capacity and makes his home at the Capital City.

HON. DAVID T. MILLER was born, May 2, 1843, near Newark, Ohio, where he resided with his parents until 1852, when they moved to Union County, Ohio, where they lived till 1856, and then moved to Iowa. He attended the common school at Sigourney, Iowa, until 1861, then entered the State University at Iowa City, where he remained until 1863, when he entered the army as a private in Company G, Fifteenth Iowa, and served until the close of the war. He then returned and entered the normal school, after which he engaged in teaching school. Then he devoted his attention to reading law, and was admitted to the bar at Ottumwa, Iowa, in 1871. He began the practice of law at that place in 1872, where he resided until 1891, when he came to Idaho, in March, 1891, and was engaged for one year in making a preliminary survey for a railroad from Boise City to Butte, Mont. Returning in 1892, entered upon the practice of law at Boise City, and was nominated and elected by the Republican party for member of the lower house of the legislature. He was elected Speaker of the House with but little opposition, and after conducting that body of the legislature successfully, he again opened his law office and is now engaged in practice, and is also negotiating sales of gold mines.

HON. GEORGE H. STEWART was born in Connersville, Ind., in the year 1858. He remained with his parents on a farm until he was fifteen years of age, when he entered the Northern Indiana Normal School at Valparaiso, graduating from the scientific and law departments in 1880. Mr. Stewart entered upon the practice of his profession at Fowler, Ind., where he Commanded a good clientage until, on account of failing health, a change of climate became necessary. After spending some time in travel, he located at Stockville, Neb., where he remained until the drought of 1890, when he removed to Boise City, Idaho. In Nebraska, Mr. Stewart held the office of Prosecuting Attorney, and was recognized as a most vigorous and fearless prosecutor. He was elected to the State Senate from Ada County, Idaho, at the recent election, and has filled that position with honor to himself and his constituents. He is looked up to as an attorney of ability and influence.

HON. CHARLES HUNT, member of the Idaho Legislature from Shoshone County, was born in Youngstown, Ohio, in 1867. He came to Idaho in 1886 and settled in Kingston, Shoshone County, where he has been engaged in lumbering the greater part of the time. Although but twenty-five years of age, he has been very active in the political struggles of his party. He is a sterling Democrat and was elected from the famous Cœur d'Alene country after one of the most bitter campaigns that section has ever known. In the legislature he has proved to be a faithful worker and has acquitted himself with honor alike to his constituents and party.

HON. L. E. WORKMAN, member of the present Idaho Legislature, was born near Mount Vernon, Knox County, Ohio, June 18, 1864. When four years of age he emigrated with his parents to Iowa, where he resided for six years. They then changed their place of residence to Republic County, Kansas, where they engaged in farming. Young Workman obtained a liberal education and in the meantime was admitted to the practice of law. He came to Idaho in 1890, and took up his residence and began practicing his profession at Idaho City. Mr. Workman served the people of Boise County as representative in the Second Legislature of Idaho in an able and fitting manner. He is liberal in his political and religious views and pronounced in his belief of equal rights. He is a strong believer in internal improvement as a means of assisting the development of the wonderful resources of his state, and took a strong stand in aid of the state in the wagon-road enterprises in which the legislature of 1893 played a liberal hand.

HON. ADDISON A. CRANE was born in Douglas County, Ore., June 16, 1862. He was educated in the public schools of that state and the Bishop Scott Grammar School of Portland. Studied law in Portland, Ore., and has been engaged in the mining business for several years in Montana and Idaho. Came to Kootenai County three years ago, and located in the town of Harrison, at which place he now resides. He is a member of the present state legislature and an officer on Governor McConnell's staff with the rank of Lieutenant Colonel. Mr. Crane distinguished himself during the last session of the legislature, not only in the amount of work accomplished, but in the able manner in which he conducted his official position.

HON. JOHN MERRILL was born in Cincinnati, Ohio, Feb. 13, 1834. When but a few weeks old his father and mother moved to West Virginia, where young Merrill was reared until seventeen years of age. In 1851 he went to St. Joe, Mo., where he resided for years, after which he crossed the plains to Oregon. The following spring he went to Siskiyou County, California, remaining there till 1861. He then went to the Oro Fino mining district and then to the Boise Basin, where he engaged in the mercantile business. After an absence of several years in California and New Mexico he returned to Boise County, Idaho, where he has since lived. Mr. Merrill is at present a member of the Idaho Legislature.

HON. GREEN WHITE, an active member of the Idaho Senate, was born in Lafayette County, Missouri, July 13, 1839. In 1849 he accompanied his mother and grandfather to California, where he attended public and private school until 1855, when he spent three years at Santa Clara College. He read law, and in 1860 moved to Walla Walla. For a number of years he was engaged in mining and merchandising in the Boise Basin. In 1888, when Elmore County was created, Mr. White was appointed Sheriff by Governor Stevenson. He served in that capacity till 1890, at which time Idaho was made a state and Mr. White was selected to represent his county in the State Senate. He was re-elected to that position in 1892.

HON. S. A. ANDERSON, member of the Idaho Legislature from Latah County, was born in Skaraborgs Län, Sweden, in 1861, and emigrated to the United States in 1880. He located at Watonwan County, Minnesota. Residing in that state but a short time, he emigrated to the Pacific Coast following various pursuits giving him a practical knowledge of the different industries of the West. He settled in Idaho in 1887, where he has since been engaged in the saw-mill and mercantile business. Mr Anderson was elected to the legislature on the Republican ticket, and served as chairman of the Committee on Ways and Means. He makes his home at Vollmer, Idaho.

HON. ROBERT NEILL was born in Henry County, Kentucky. He was educated at the University of Kentucky. In 1875 he went to the Black Hills, passing through the hardships common to that country. He was married in 1879, and came to Northern Idaho in 1882, where he has accumulated a most comfortable home. He is a member of the present legislature, which position he has admirably and acceptably filled. Mr. Neill is a great grandson of Col. John Green of Revolutionary fame.

HON. D. V. STEPHENS is a native of Springfield, Clark County, Ohio where he was born, Nov. 19, 1854. In 1859 he moved with his parents to Kansas, where he resided for a number of years. He was for a long period employed in the transportation department of the Atchison, Topeka & Santa Fe Railway. Mr. Stephens located in Idaho in 1889, near Lewiston, and has ever since been more or less connected with the Democratic party of the state. He was elected a member of the Idaho Legislature as joint representative for Nez Perce and Idaho counties. Mr. Stephens is an advocate of honest and just legislation.

HON. A. S. ROBERTSON, member of the legislature from Ada and Canyon counties, was born in Elgin County, Province of Ontario, Canada, Jan. 22, 1863, of Scotch parentage. Mr. Robertson lived in Whiteside County Illinois, from 1866 to 1878. He went to Fillmore County, Nebraska, in that year, and after receiving a common school and collegiate education, removed in the spring of 1882 to Arnold, Custer County, Nebraska, and organized the State Bank of Arnold, of which institution he became cashier, remaining as such until 1890. During this time he took an active part in all the political fights in that state. Selling his interest in the banking business, he went to Idaho in 1890, and is at present engaged in mercantile pursuits, mining and investments. He was elected on the Republican ticket at the last election.

HON. J. I. MITCHAM was born near Lafayette, Ind., in 1849. He went to Nebraska in 1867, and came to Idaho in 1883. He was educated at Tabor College, Iowa, and was a member of the Fifteenth Territorial Legislature of Idaho. Mr. Mitcham's extraordinary ability and the untiring interest he takes in the promotion of his county caused him to be elected State Senator from Latah County on the Republican ticket at the November election. Mr. Mitcham is an attorney by profession.

IDAHO—THE GEM OF THE MOUNTAINS.

HON. W. J. BOGARD was born in Chariton County, Missouri, in 1863. He received a limited country school education. Taking Horace Greeley's advice, he began to travel westward at the age of seventeen, and landed in Idaho in 1883. Since that time he has been engaged in farming, merchandising and at present in mining at Rocky Bar, where he has some valuable quartz claims. He is in love with the Gem of the Mountains, believing it to be the paradise of the West. In politics he has affiliated himself with the Democrats and was the choice of Elmore County for representative at the last election. He has served his county faithfully and honorably.

HON. J. J. MCCARTHY was born in the year 1864, in the "garden spot of the world," Santa Clara County, California. He spent the first years of his life in fruit raising and farming and in the meantime graduated with high honors from the Garden City Business College. In 1887 he married Miss Irene Fiedler, one of San Jose's accomplished daughters, the following year started for Idaho, and has since resided in Bonanza City, Custer County, where he has been successfully engaged in the general mercantile and mining business. He had never mixed in politics, but was nominated for the legislature and the people showed their appreciation of him, as he received over two-thirds the entire vote of his county, and had the honor of receiving the largest number of votes of any one man in the county. He has been very successful as a legislator, is as popular with the members as he is with his own people, and has made a record of which any young man should be proud.

HON. GEORGE J. LEWIS, representative from Alturas County in the Second State Legislature, is a native of Minnesota, and thirty-two years of age He was educated at the university of that state and came to Idaho in 1881 to establish the Ketchum *Keystone*, which is still a prosperous weekly newspaper. He became assistant cashier of the First National Bank of Ketchum in 1887, cashier of the same institution in 1889, and is now principal of the private banking firm of George J. Lewis, doing business at that place. Mr. Lewis' wide range of business experience, and thorough acquaintance with the mining and commercial interests of his section, render him especially fitted to represent the best interests of the state. He was elected to the legislature by a handsome majority, and received the entire support of the People's party for the speakership of the House. Taking an active interest in public affairs, Mr. Lewis is a careful student of the political and industrial questions of the day, and promises to rank with the foremost of Idaho's representative men.

HON. J. M. HOWE, born, April 30, 1845, at Hanover, Oxford County, Maine, received an academic education at Hebron in the same state. He studied law two years and emigrated to Idaho in 1869, where he has since resided. He was admitted to the Nez Perce County bar in 1870 and was Register of the Lewiston Land Office from 1877 to 1885. He was elected Mayor of the city of Lewiston in 1888, and served as City Attorney in 1891 and 1892. He was a member of the State Constitutional Convention, and is at present a member of the Idaho State Senate.

HON. ROBERT CAMPBELL is a native of the State of Wisconsin, being born on a farm there in 1854. He emigrated to Idaho in 1880, and was in the great Wood River country in its best days, since which time he has followed prospecting and mining. Mr. Campbell was always a Republican until last year, when he became a member of the Populist party, owing to its stand on silver. He was nominated and elected State Senator by the Populists in Custer County, receiving a large majority of votes cast.

HON. H. H. BANGS was born in Sierra County, California, Oct. 14, 1857. He lived in California until he was twenty years of age, when he married and came to what is now Latah County, Idaho, where he has since resided. Mr. Bangs is a farmer by occupation. He was elected to the Second Legislature on the Republican ticket, to which party he is thoroughly devoted.

HON. GILL F. FLETCHER, member of the Idaho Legislature, was born in New Hampshire in 1848. His parents removed to Iowa in 1851, where he was raised on a farm. He was married in 1868, elected Sheriff of Johnson County, Iowa, in 1883, re-elected in 1885 and again in 1887. He moved with his family to Idaho in 1888, settling in Bingham County, on the North Fork of Snake River. He was elected a member of the Second Idaho State Legislature in 1892 and was the father of the Fremont County division bill. Mr. Fletcher has always been a staunch Democrat.

HON. RALPH A. COWDEN was born in Iowa City, Iowa, in 1865, but was raised at Clinton in the same state. In 1883 he moved to Denver and engaged in the lumber business, and in the following year took up his residence in Caldwell, Idaho, where he has followed the lumber business ever since. He was elected joint representative, last November, of Ada and Elmore Counties. Mr. Cowden's business has never allowed him to mingle very much in the political arena, but his record as a representative was very complimentary not only to himself but to the counties he represented.

HON. R. A. CALDWELL was born in Warren County, Illinois, Sept. 4, 1851. He has spent nearly his entire life in the stock business, and came to Idaho in the year 1880 to increase his capacity in that line. In 1890, when Idaho became a state, he was elected to the First Legislature and was re-elected to represent his county at the second term. Mr. Caldwell has done much to further the interests of the "Gem State," and his efforts are duly appreciated by the people.

HON. E. J. TURNER came from the Badger State to Montana in 1866, where he spent five years in the mines, being more or less successful. He then moved to the State of Washington and settled in the vicinity of Medical Lake in the fall of 1871, being one of the earliest pioneers of that section. The failure of Jay Cooke, together with the outbreak of the Nez Perce Indians under Chief Joseph, caused him to remove to Southern Idaho in 1877. He is now proprietor of the Spring Brook Stock Ranch, one of the largest in Southern Idaho, and is extensively engaged in the cattle business.

HON. AARON F. PARKER was born in the western part of England, March 16, 1856. He received a grammar school education and at the age of twelve years embarked in a seafaring life, which he followed for six years, being engaged in trading on the western coast of South America, in the Rio de la Plata, on the eastern coast, and also in the West India Islands. From 1873 to 1875 he was employed in the city of London. In 1876 Mr. Parker sailed for San Francisco, whence he finally drifted to Idaho, and for several years led a most adventurous life as miner, prospector and Indian fighter in the mountains of that state and Eastern Oregon. He served with the United States troops in the Indian campaigns of 1877-78-79 as scout, courier and guide, and also acted incidentally as war correspondent of several metropolitan newspapers. In 1880 he established, at Lewiston, Idaho, a newspaper called the *Nez Perce News*, which he edited with marked ability until the breaking out of the Cœur d'Alene excitement, when he sold the *News* and left for the mines. He was one of the first twenty-five men to enter the camp in September, 1883, and was the original discoverer of the high gold-bearing gravel deposits which are now known as the Old Wash Channel. In the early spring of 1884 he established at Eagle City the *Cœur d'Alene Eagle*. He was also postmaster at Eagle City during the summer of 1884. In the spring of 1885 he again assumed control of the *Nez Perce News*, and in June, 1886, established the *Idaho Free Press* at Grangeville, Idaho County, which is now one of the foremost papers in the state and a power for good in advertising the wonderful wealth of that great county. His only appearance in public life was as a member of the State Constitutional Convention, where he won golden opinions by his knowledge of fundamental principles. Mr. Parker is one of the rising men of the State of Idaho.

COL. J. E. MILLER, joint senator from Owyhee and Cassia counties, was born in Pennsylvania, in the year 1842. He entered the Army of the Potomac as a private soldier in 1861, where he participated in many of the most important engagements, receiving successive promotions for meritorious conduct. During his service he was at times severely wounded, from the effects of which he has never recovered. In 1869 he followed the tide of emigration to the West, and, drifting toward the setting sun, in 1877 found himself a resident of the far-famed and beautiful valley of Goose Creek, in what is now Cassia County. Colonel Miller has stood steadfast with the land of his adoption, has grown with its growth, and by his great energy and attention to duty has done more for his constituents than any of his predecessors.

HON. JAMES W. BALLANTINE was born in 1839, at Pittsburgh, Pa. He was graduated from the public schools of Pittsburgh. He entered the army as a private in 1861 and was mustered out in 1865 as a Lieutenant Colonel. From 1865 to 1883 he was engaged in the oil-refining business in Pennsylvania. In the spring of 1883 he came to the Pacific Coast to take charge of a mining and smelting business at Muldoon, Alturas County. Colonel Ballantine has taken an active interest in politics since he became of age. He was twice elected to the Pennsylvania Legislature. At the last election he was sent to the Idaho Legislature from Alturas County, on the Populist ticket, by an overwhelming majority, and endeavored to legislate in the interests of the people by reducing expenses, in guarding the treasury as far as possible from the raids made by the party in power.

HON. G. F. YEARIAN was born in Perry County, Illinois, in 1858, and in 1864, when only six years of age, crossed the plains with his parents with ox-teams to Montana. In 1872 he moved to Idaho, where he received a limited country school education, and is now one of the many successful miners and stock growers of this state. In politics he early in life affiliated with the Republican party, and was, at the November election of 1892, chosen representative from Lemhi County, and served his district faithfully, with honor and credit to himself and constituents.

HON. JAMES J. STORY was born in Virginia in 1834. He went to California in 1852 and engaged in mining. From there he went to Nevada in 1873 and then came to Idaho in 1881, where he again engaged in mining. He was elected to the House of Representatives on the Republican ticket and served in that capacity during the Second Legislature. Mr. Story is at present engaged in the business of private banking.

HON. H. F. MCCARTER was born in Grayson County, Virginia. He came West in 1886, to Alturas County, Idaho, and engaged in stock raising, which business he still follows. He received an academic education in Grayson County, Virginia. At the last general election he was elected to the legislature on the Populist ticket, by an overwhelming majority. He was formerly a Jeffersonian Democrat. He at present resides at Corral, Logan County, Idaho.

HON. F. C. MOSS, State Senator from Ada County, was born in Belvidere, Illinois, in 1852, and came to Wyoming in 1873, where he was engaged in stock raising and contracting for ten years. He moved to Idaho, and has been engaged in the general merchandise business at Payette for the past ten years. In the fall of 1892 he was the only Democrat elected from his county on the legislative ticket.

HON. T. W. GIBTON of Grangeville, Idaho, was born in West Virginia in 1832. He lived at Lay Harp, Hancock County, Illinois, until 1852, when he came to the Pacific Coast and visited the states of Oregon and California until 1861. He then came to Oro Fino, Idaho, and engaged in mining until 1869. He located on a ranch near Grangeville, Idaho County, and at present is engaged in stock raising. He was elected to the Eleventh Territorial Legislature, and was later elected to the Second State Legislature on the Democratic ticket by a large majority. He was engaged in mining and prospecting, and discovered the famous Lemhi Mine, in Lemhi County, in 1866.

IDAHO—THE GEM OF THE MOUNTAINS.

Hon. Fred T. Dubois, United States Senator for Idaho, was born in Crawford County, Illinois, on the twenty-ninth of May, 1851. His father, Jesse K. Dubois, familiarly known throughout the state as "Uncle Jesse," was one of President Lincoln's warmest friends, and had it not been for the President's assassination, would have held a cabinet portfolio during the President's second term. The subject of this sketch was the youngest son of the family, and inherited in a large measure his father's political proclivities, and even as a boy displayed marked ability in the management of local politics in Springfield. Every care was bestowed upon his education, and after a thorough training in the public schools of Springfield and special courses under private tutors, he was sent to Yale, from which college he was graduated in 1872. After his return from college he went to Chicago and accepted a clerkship in a wholesale house, where he remained until appointed to a position in the State Auditor's office in Springfield. This appointment again brought him into politics, and gave him prominence in political affairs in that section, and it was not long till he was appointed Secretary of the Board of Railway and Warehouse Commissioners in Illinois. In 1880, he started for Idaho, reaching Blackfoot in August. He was appointed United States Marshal of Idaho in 1882. This office he held until September 1, 1886. He was made a successful candidate for delegate to the Fiftieth Congress by both Republicans and anti-Mormons. Mr. Dubois was re-elected to the Fifty-first Congress over James H. Hawley and Judge Black, and his term of office expired March 4, 1891. He was complimented with being chosen one of the first United States senators to represent the Gem State in Congress. He is at present acting in that capacity and his efforts are applauded by the citizens of his state. Mr. Dubois must be credited with being a most prominent figure in the admission of Idaho as a State.

Col. John Green.—In illustrating the old fort of Boise Barracks, and speaking of the early history of Idaho, which includes the famous Bannock and Nez Perce Indian wars of 1877 and 1878, it would be unjust to omit the name of that gallant and popular soldier, Col. John Green, United States Army, retired. Although a retired army officer at present, Colonel Green spent forty-three years of his life in active service, having risen from the ranks to a commander of a regiment and engaged in many a hard fought battle. Colonel Green was born in Wurtemburg, Germany, in 1825, and came to America at the age of seven years. His father worked a farm in Ohio, where young Green assisted him. This occupation did not suit the young man and he sought other employment, when he came in contact with a recruiting officer for a mounted rifle company which was to make a trip to Oregon. Green enlisted, and from that time dates his military record. He was active in the Mexican and the late Civil War and the Indian wars in the various parts of the United States, of which Idaho had her share. Colonel Green has been stationed at several Western posts, but Boise Barracks has long been his headquarters, and after his retirement he adopted Boise City as his home. Colonel Green is not only a favorite among the soldiers, but his society is sought by the best citizens within his vicinity.

Hon. Stephen A. Fenn was born near Watertown, Conn., March 8, 1820. His father moved with his family to Western New York in 1824. He received an academic education and studied law in Buffalo, N. Y. He removed to Iowa in 1844, where he was married in 1847. Went to California, "across the plains," in 1850, where he was joined by his wife two years later. Came to the Salmon River mines, then in Washington Territory, in July, 1862, making his home in Florence, Idaho County. He practiced law and served one term as District Judge in Nez Perce County and was appointed first Register of the United States Land Office in the Lewiston district in 1867. Mr. Fenn represented Idaho County several times in the legislature, serving as Speaker of the House of Representatives and later as President of the Council. In 1874 he was elected a delegate to Congress from the Territory of Idaho and re-elected two years later. He retired from active political life at the close of his second term in Congress and now lives on his farm in Idaho County. He suffered a stroke of paralysis in 1889, from which he never recovered, and died Dec. 9, 1892.

James H. Wallis, editor of the Post, was born at London, Eng., on the thirteenth day of April, 1861, a few hours after the first gun was fired on Fort Sumter, at the opening of the Civil War. His boyhood was spent in the Tower of London, where his father occupied a position under the English Government, and of which historical place his grandfather held the important office of turnkey. Mr. Wallis came to the United States in 1880, arriving in Salt Lake City, Utah, on the fifth day of May of that year. He was editor of a newspaper when he was twenty years old, and has owned three newspapers since that time. While editing the Nephi (Utah) Ensign, he was arrested for libel. He wished to leave the Provo (Utah) Morning Dispatch, the first paper in Utah to leave the People's party and come out squarely for division and the Democratic party. He was elected Prosecuting Attorney for Juab County, Utah, when but twenty-seven years of age, being a successful lawyer as we, as a bright journalist. Before he was twenty years of age he had written over 100 poems, of great merit, and Tullidge in his "History of Utah" refers to him as the "Boy Poet of Utah." Mr. Wallis is a devoted disciple of Jefferson, and one of the brightest Democratic editors in the State of Idaho. He was managing editor of the Ogden (Utah) Daily Post before moving to Montpelier. He is a member of the Mormon Church, occupying the ecclesiastical position of a "seventy," and it was his faith in his religion that induced him to leave his native country and gather with the main body of the church. He was married when twenty years of age, to Miss Elizabeth Todd, of London, and has an interesting family of eight children as a result of their happy union, four boys and four girls. Mr. Wallis is a self-taught man, never having been to school since he was nine years of age. His parents were poor and he has had to work for his own living since that time.

Hon. John C. Greaves, member of the legislature from Oneida County, was born in Salt Lake City, Utah, in 1855. While quite young he moved with his parents to Logan, Utah, and lived with them until he reached the age of twenty-two, at which time he married the daughter of C. W. Card, one of the pioneers of Cache Valley. Mr. Greaves having learned the carpenter trade, followed that pursuit for eight years. Having a desire for more room and land than could be acquired in the city, he with his wife and three small children moved to Preston, Oneida County, Idaho, his present home. Here he was elected Precinct Justice of the Peace and succeeded himself two years later. He is now, and has been for the past four years, Postmaster at Preston, and is also engaged in the merchandise business at that place.

Hon. Frank A. Fenn was born in Nevada County, California, Sept. 11, 1853. He came to Idaho with his father's family in 1862, and has made it his home ever since. He was educated in the public schools of the territory and at the United States Naval Academy at Annapolis, Md., having been appointed a naval cadet by Hon. J. K. Shafer, delegate in Congress, in 1869. Mr. Fenn returned to Idaho in 1865 and engaged in teaching, and later in farming and stock raising. He was elected a member of the Territorial House of Representatives in 1886 from Idaho County, and was also a member of the First State Legislature, serving as speaker of the House. Since that time he has been engaged in the State Land Department.

Hon. J. G. Watts was born in Wellsboro, Pa., July 25, 1858. He lost his father in the Civil War in April, 1863. He was educated at the Soldiers Orphan School and State Normal School at Mansfield Pa., and taught in the public schools for five years and in Petersburg, Ill., three years. Mr. Watts studied law in the office of F. W. McNeely at Petersburg, Ill., while teaching there, and was admitted to practice at North Platte, Neb., April 1, 1886. He practiced in Nebraska four years, the last two at Omaha; came to Idaho in July, 1890, and located at Idaho City. He was elected to the State Senate from Boise County at the November election in 1891.

Hon. H. F. Johnson was born in Indiana, Nov. 2, 1830, and removed to Missouri when but a small boy. He lived in Carthage, the county seat of Jasper County, until May 1, 1853, when he started across the plains for Oregon with an ox team. He reached Fosters, across the Cascade Mountains, the second day of October. He settled in Lane County in the spring of 1854. The following fall he went to the mines and has been engaged in mining and prospecting more or less ever since. Mr. Johnson came to Idaho in April, 1864, and has been prospecting in the state since that time. He was a Republican in politics up to Hayes' election, when he left both the old parties, disgusted. When the People's party came to the surface he joined it and was nominated at the party convention for State Senator from Washington County, and was elected by a handsome majority.

Hon. W. Cleveinger, member of the legislature from Payette, Ada County, Idaho, was born in Green County, Pennsylvania, in 1836, and came to Northern Missouri in 1865, where he was raised on a farm. He came to the State of Idaho in 1882 and engaged in stock raising and the lumber business. He was elected to the Second State Legislature from Ada County as a Republican by a large majority.

Hon. J. S. Barrett, member of the legislature from Bear Lake County, Idaho, was born in London, Eng., Feb. 8, 1854. He came to America in 1864 with a sister and mother, his father having died when he was but four years old. He took up a home in Utah with friends of his parents and served as chore boy on a farm for a number of years; then accepted a position as teamster for a freighting outfit. Soon afterward he was placed in charge of the outfit, with an office near Salt Lake City. He was married in 1876, and since that time has followed school teaching and acted as manager for a mercantile and contracting company up to 1888, when he embarked in business for himself at Montpelier, Idaho, where he now lives. He has occupied various public positions and enjoys politics, although not a professional politician.

Hon. H. H. Clay, the representative from Logan County, Idaho, was born in Lake County, Illinois, within a short distance of the present location of the World's Fair, in 1855, and came to Idaho in 1879. Mr. Clay is a Republican in politics, was a member of the Fifteenth Territorial Legislature and is a member of the Second Legislature of the State of Idaho. His popularity is such that he was the only Republican member elected from Logan County. He is at present engaged in the mercantile and mining business at Bellevue. Mr. Clay is the owner of the Redwing and Gate City mines, which he has bonded for $10,900.

Hon. Frank L. Ruggan was born in Bluffton, Ind., Jan. 1, 1864. He graduated from the Bluffton High School in 1883, and commenced the practice of law, in 1887, in Bluffton. He moved to Cœur d'Alene, Idaho, and opened a law office there in April, 1890. He was one of the founders of the Cœur d'Alene Press in February, 1891. He was elected on the Republican ticket to the Second Idaho Legislature, and was a hard worker in the interest of his section of the state. He is a man of energy, and has every prospect of a bright future in the State of Idaho.

CANYON ABOVE GREAT SHOSHONE FALLS.

GREAT TWIN FALLS, SNAKE RIVER

OFFICERS' ROW, FORT SHERMAN.

STOCK RANCH ON THE ST JOE RIVER, KOOTENAI COUNTY.

IDAHO FALLS.

The Centre of a Rich and Prolific Irrigated District.

RESOURCES OF A MAGIC CITY.

The accompanying map, showing the wonderful canal system, and the engravings illustrating the magnificent buildings at Idaho Falls, will portray to the person who may glance at this souvenir what this town is at present and what may be her chances for the future. But we deem it necessary to publish a few statements giving the resources of a young city that has become famous and gained complimentary notoriety in more ways than one. Idaho Falls is situated in the eastern part of the "Gem State," at the point where the Union Pacific Railway crosses Snake River, which will be seen by reference to the map of the entire state, printed in this number. It is about midway between Denver, Col., and Portland, Ore., and is but 72 miles from America's great Yellowstone Park. It is also situated upon the great "thermal belt" around the world, strange as it may seem, upon which are located all the most populous and enterprising cities in the world.

The climate within the vicinity of Idaho Falls is equal to any in Idaho, which, as is shown by statistics in this work, is the best in the world.

While we could refer the reader to the special article on Bingham County, in which the town is located, for general information, it will be well to refer slightly to the stock-raising and agricultural industries tributary to the Falls city. At present, stock raising—cattle, horses and sheep—is the chief industry. This is carried on very extensively, as the grasses here are par excellence. Agriculturists are, however, crowding into this country, and with the extension of the immense system of canals and ditches, every acre of the land under them will be in the hands of industrious farmers, and what can now be entered at a nominal price as government land, will, with the water, be worth from $20 to $100 per acre.

In the vicinity of this rapidly growing city may be found immense quantities of timber, coal and stone. The coal veins in the Snake River Valley, not many miles distant, run from 9 to 22 feet in thickness. About six miles to the east of Idaho Falls there is an immense volcanic deposit known as the "Red Rock Quarry." This rock is of a beautiful desired red, and can be cut with common edged tools into any shape, when first extracted, but after being exposed to the air for say three or four weeks, it becomes hard as granite and has a resistance of 22 tons to the cubic foot, or about two tons greater than ordinary pressed brick. It has been said that this quarry contains enough of this handsome red stone to build a city the size of Chicago.

The land here is exceptionally prolific. There are to be seen fields of wheat to yield from 60 to 80 bushels per acre, oats and vegetables in proportion, and alfalfa, three cuttings, aggregating from seven to ten tons per acre.

Two bright and spirited newspapers, the Times and the Register, are published at Idaho Falls, samples of which may be had upon application.

The water power at Idaho Falls is estimated by the United States Government Engineer at 126,000 horse power, or more than double the water power at Spokane Falls, Wash. This has partially been utilized and now turns the wheels of the immense patent roller flouring mill located here. Numerous factories are figuring upon locating here, owing to the capacity of water power and the cheerful outlook for Idaho Falls to become a great city.

The people of this prosperous town are responsible for its unparalleled promotion. They are thrifty, enterprising, and encourage all deserving propositions, no matter how small or large.

Many fine buildings may be seen located at Idaho Falls. The handsome Teton Hotel, the stately Odd Fellows Orphans Home, the commodious High School building, the immense mercantile houses of the Consolidated Implement Company, Anderson Bros. and the Co-operative Wagon and Machine Company, the Idaho Falls Roller Mills, etc., all add to the metropolitan appearance of this magic city. The Governmental Experimental Farm and the United States Signal Service Station for Idaho are located here.

The location of canals for irrigating purposes is most admirably chosen and capable of furnishing an abundance of water to cover from 500,000 to 5,000,000 acres, only requiring to be extended. The water, which is obtained from Snake River, is of immense quantity and, at the present ordinary flow, sufficient to irrigate 500,000 acres, and the storing facilities for irrigating 5,000,000 acres are almost limitless on the Upper Snake, at a nominal cost. There are 2,500,000 acres of valley land surrounding Idaho Falls which is all available for agriculture; and when it is understood that no country in the world that depends upon natural rainfall can begin to compare with the country that depends upon irrigation, what may be expected of the future of Idaho Falls? Over $1,000,000 has been expended during the last two years in building canals near this town. Men of influence and capital have become interested in the irrigation of this district, which speaks well for continued prosperity in the Idaho Falls country. The statement which follows shows 300 miles of mains in operation or in course of construction near Idaho Falls:

*MAIN CANALS.	Estimated number acres wild land cultivated in 1891.	Acres under cultivation.	Acres of land under canal.	Number of miles completed.	Cost of construction.	Capital stock.	Depth capacity, number of feet.	Width at bottom, number of feet.	Length, completed, miles.
Idaho Canal System	2,500	10,000	100,000	60	$150,000	$250,000	5	40	9
Great Western System	5,000	2,000	75,000	30	120,000	180,000	6	40 to 60	8
Eagle Rock and Willow Creek System	5,000	25,000	50,000	45	90,000	100,000	5	8	45
Idaho Falls Canal System	7,000	1,000	75,000	30	150,000	250,000	3	15	8
Butte and Market Lake		1,000	2,000	25	60,000	60,000	4	25	8
Harrison Canal		15,000	10,000	35	15,000		4	28	15
Farmer's Friend		4,500	12,000	35	15,000		4	30	12
Burgess Canal		3,500	6,000	15	6,000		5	25	15
Parks Canal	3,000	7,000	5,000	10	10,000		3	22	8
Anthem Canal	2,000	3,500	25,000	20	8,000		4	8	8
Long Island Canal	8,000	8,000	35,000	20			3	8	12
Totals	75,000	80,300	450,000	279	$800,000	$1,000,000			381

* Complete figures not obtainable regarding the smaller canals.

‡ Including three branches, 12 to 16 feet at bottom, 3 to 3 feet deep; to be completed next July.

The projected railroads connecting the Falls are the extension of the Chicago & Northwestern from Fort Casper, in Wyoming, to Boise City, and the Pacific Coast on the west, and the proposed branches of the Union Pacific system to the Yellowstone Park and the line to Challis and Salmon City to the northwest.

The Union Pacific system—the Oregon Short Line and the Utah & Northern branch—now supplies all railroad facilities to Idaho Falls running north and south over the only practicable rail route afforded by the configuration of the country for over 500 miles each way between the northern and southern boundaries of the United States.

In conclusion, it would require a visit to Idaho Falls to become thoroughly acquainted with her unlimited resources. Correspondence is solicited, and information will be cheerfully rendered by

R. ROUNDS,
Secretary Board of Trade, Idaho Falls, Idaho.

SNAKE RIVER FRUIT FARM.

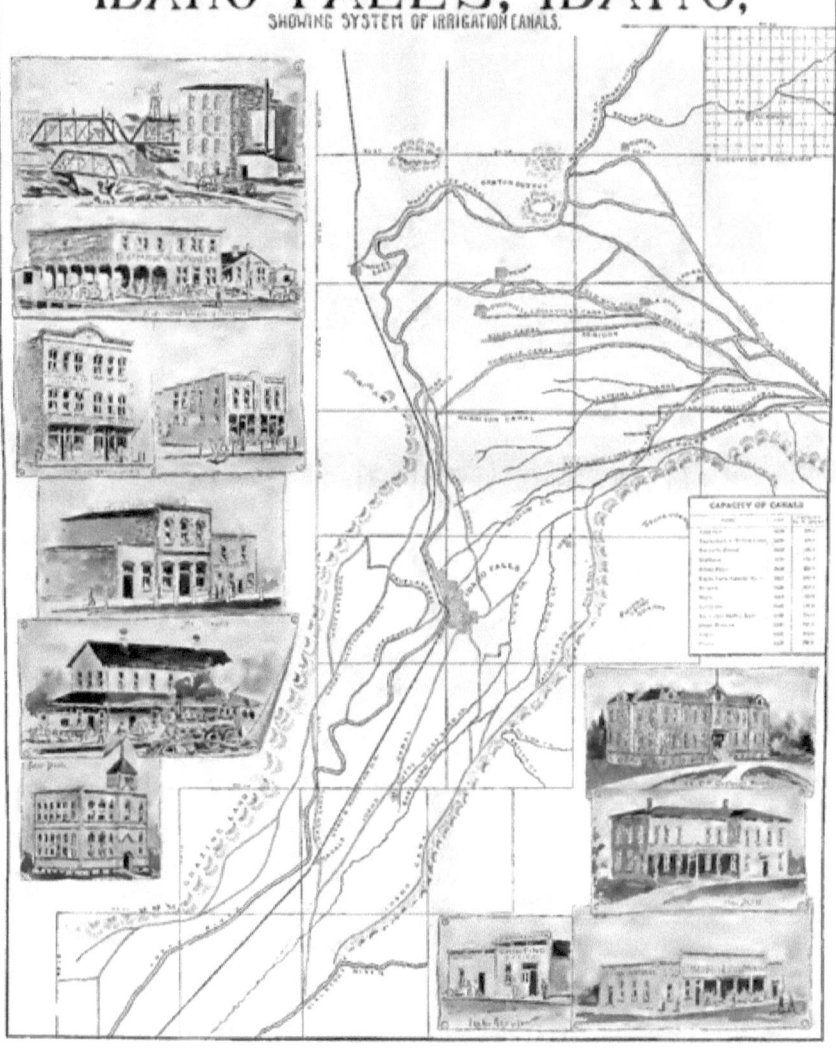

UPPER SNAKE RIVER VALLEY
AND THE COUNTRY TRIBUTARY TO
IDAHO FALLS, IDAHO,
SHOWING SYSTEM OF IRRIGATION CANALS.

CŒUR D'ALENE CITY.

Ⴑhҽ Ⴑisϲonsiη Ⴅentral Ⴑiηҽs

N. P. R. R. CO. LESSEE

FOR DETAILED INFORMATION
CALL ON OR ADDRESS

The
World's Fair
Route...

 ANDING passengers at the
Grand Central Station,
CHICAGO. from which
Station passengers can
take trains for WORLD'S
FAIR GROUNDS. The Grand Cen-
tral Depot also contains 200 rooms
for guests, and is the most elegant
Railroad Station in this country.

C. E. STONE
Passenger and Ticket Agent
ST. PAUL, MINN.

JAS. C. POND
General Passenger and Ticket Agent
CHICAGO, ILL.

❀ ❀ ❀ ❀ ❀

The Wisconsin Central Line—The World's Fair Route

THE UNION PACIFIC SYSTEM.

A Description of the Main Line and Branches, Junction Points, Connections, Trains and Equipment.

This great national highway is so well known, not only throughout the United States, but all over the world, that a mere reference to it would seem sufficient; yet for the benefit of those who have never had the pleasure of riding over its smooth track, and thus had an opportunity of gazing upon the fine scenery along its route, the following description is given:

It formed a part of the first transcontinental line of railroad from ocean to ocean, and was conceived, and its construction authorized, as a war measure, the needs of the government during the War of the Rebellion having clearly shown the necessity for it. When first talked of many thought the feat of constructing a line of railroad over the Rocky Mountains an utter impossibility. Many of those who had crossed the plains, deserts and mountains to California in '49-50 knew very well a railroad could not be built there, for "How could a locomotive ascend a mountain where six yoke of oxen could scarcely haul a wagon?" It must be remembered that the line of this road follows almost exactly the old emigrant wagon road, not only on the plains on the north side of the Platte River, through the State of Nebraska, but in fact all the way to Ogden, in Utah Territory. In the days of '49-50, when long trains of gold seekers, after outfitting at Council Bluffs, wended their way over the plains, the country was filled with hostile Indians, herds of wild buffalo, deer and antelope. There was scarcely a house west of the Elkhorn River, within 20 miles of Omaha. Now the traveler sits in a luxurious Pullman car, and is whirled over the smooth railroad at 60 miles an hour, past villages, towns and cities filled with active, busy, intelligent people, and as far as the eye can reach on either side of the road farms join each other. A million and a half of people live in the State of Nebraska, through which the road runs.

The last spike, making the union of the two roads, the Union Pacific and the Central Pacific, was driven at Promontory, just beyond Salt Lake, in May, 1869.

Years have demonstrated that this grand road was most wisely and skillfully planned. There is no other line to-day possessing its peculiar advantages, and there can never be a railway constructed across the continent like it, for the simple reason that the Union Pacific occupies the very best belt of country obtainable. There is immunity, on the one hand, from the blazing suns and stifling alkali dust of the Southern deserts; and on the other, the lightest possible snowfall to be encountered on the mountain summits. It is the natural highway, either for summer or winter, spring or autumn, and it must forever remain so. No amount of specious reasoning can shake the solid fact that the Union Pacific line is the one railway across the continent unassailable by summer heat or winter storms.

This railway, "The World's Pictorial Line," is one of the very best on this continent. Its four main stems, one from Kansas City, one from Leavenworth, one from Sioux City, and one from Council Bluffs and Omaha, uniting at Cheyenne and diverging again at Green River, one for Portland and one for San Francisco, are crowded with the commerce of the Orient and the Occident, while people from every nation in the world may be seen on its passenger trains. Every improvement which human ingenuity has invented for the safety or comfort of the traveler is in use on the Union Pacific; Solid Vestibuled Trains, Pullman Palace Sleeping and Dining Cars, Reclining Chair Cars, Colonist Sleeping Cars and Union Depots. These magnificent trains are lighted with the very latest invention in railway car illumination, the Pintsch Gas Light System. For nearly 500 miles west of Council Bluffs and 700 miles west of Kansas City there are no heavy grades or curves. The Pacific Hotel Company manage the eating-houses, under the supervision of the railway company, and no better meals are to be found on any railroad in the United States. A luxurious dining-car service is maintained from Kansas City and Omaha to Denver, and from Omaha to Portland and San Francisco.

Crossing the Missouri River from the transfer depot, Council Bluffs, over a magnificent steel bridge of 11 spans, 75 feet above the water, each span 250 feet long, resting upon immense stone piers, Omaha is reached, or, crossing the Missouri River at Sioux City over a fine steel bridge, thence to Columbus, Neb., and

THE TRIP ACROSS THE CONTINENT

to either Portland or San Francisco commences. Leaving Omaha, the metropolis of Nebraska, with a population of 150,000, the road follows the Platte River through the thickly settled and fertile Platte Valley and crosses mile after mile of level country, as impressive to those unfamiliar with such scenes as is the unbounded level of the ocean.

Fremont, 47 miles west of Omaha, is a city of 6,665 inhabitants. Columbus, 45 miles further on, has 3,950 people. Grand Island, 62 miles further west, has 8,000 people; 40 miles further west is Kearney, with 8,600 inhabitants. North Platte, 291 miles west of Omaha, with 3,134 inhabitants; Sidney is 123 miles further, with 1,412 people, and has a large military post, and next is Cheyenne (516 miles from Omaha), the capital of Wyoming, population 12,744. At this point the Kansas Main Line via Denver connects with the Nebraska Main Line from Council Bluffs.

Leaving Kansas City, population 132,416, situated at the junction of the Kaw or Kansas River with the Missouri, via the Kansas Main Line of the Union Pacific System, one passes through some of the finest farming land of the West and a succession of thriving cities and towns. And so it may be told of every branch of the Union Pacific. They traverse the scenic, agricultural, horticultural and mining centres of the United States, and the equipments are such that every comfort is afforded to the traveler to visit a new and prosperous country.

 DAHO "THE GEM OF THE MOUNTAINS"

CAN·BE VISITED BY TAKING . . . . . .

The Wonderland Route

NORTHERN PACIFIC RAILROAD

Daily
Through
Trains FROM CHICAGO

VESTIBULE
TRAIN
SERVICE—NONE BETTER

TO ALL PROMINENT POINTS IN THE West

THE BEST DINING AND
FINEST SLEEPING CARS

STOP AT

THE NATIONAL PLEASURE RESORT

A better trip than this and through to the Pacific Coast cannot be
devised as a suitable companion to a visit to the World's Fair.
Full information as to rates, etc., can be obtained by calling at
the offices of the Northern Pacific and Wisconsin Central Lines in
——————— Chicago or addressing ———————

J. M. HANNAFORD,
General Traffic Manager,
ST. PAUL, MINN.

CHAS. S. FEE,
General Passenger and Ticket Agent,
ST. PAUL, MINN.

IDAHO STATE UNIVERSITY, MOSCOW.